Broken Cycle

By: Maria Stollenwerck

The evening rain that fell like meteors splashing into the earth became heavier as Essence walked into Randy's Bar. It was a Monday night and although her goal was to only drink on weekends, her day consumed with teaching middle schoolers, immediately made her say, "Fuck that." Randy's Bar was on the corner of Cornell, down the street from all the neighborhood grocery stores. Essence walked up to the empty bar and sat down, shaking off her umbrella, and removing her jacket. She was dressed casually, and the bottom of her navy blue slacks were soaked from a puddle she stepped in. Her cream colored blouse had a V-neck shape, just barely showing the small chest tattoo she had that read: *Carpe Diem.*

The lights in the bar were dim, with a brownish, burnt orange and cranberry tint to it. The windows were huge, nearly touching the ceiling, and only 2 feet from the floor. The maroon colored blinds were slightly opened, and you could see the rain coming down hard. The floors were made up of different colored tiles in shades of blues, browns, and tan. The bar's counter was positioned in an unfinished circular shape, housing many bottles of alcohol, and wine that were neatly lined against the wall, or shelved. There were chairs made of chestnut wood and cushioned for seating outside the counter. On the wall behind the bar, there is a painting of a boat sailing the ocean at dusk. A bird is flying above the boat, blocking what's left of the setting sun. There's a quote at the bottom of the painting that reads: *Life goes on.*

She took a deep breath and called for the waiter. "Excuse me," she said. When he turned around, Essence quietly chuckled to herself, covering her mouth with her freshly manicured nails. "What's funny?" he asked with a smirk. "Nothing. I didn't expect you to be so handsome when you turned around," He blushed, and asked, "What can I get for you young lady?" Essence glared at him, smiled and said, "Double shot of tequila." "On a Monday huh? Rough day?" Essence, taken aback by his curiosity, replied, "Actually, yea. Yea it was a rough day." She took her shots, sat her glass down, and stared at the bartender. He stared back, seemingly asking many questions without uttering a single word to her. Essence giggled. "Why are you staring at me like that?" The bartender gazed into her brown eyes and answered, "I'm just curious to know how to turn your rough day into a better evening." She laughed. Covering her mouth again and asked for another shot. "We can start with another shot and see where the night goes." The bartender obliged, pouring another double shot, this time adding a glass of water with it. "Take your time sweetheart," he said. Essence smiled. "What's your name?"

"Essence." she replied.

"Essence? I like that."

"And yours?"

"I'm Isaiah," he answered.

"Isaiah?"

"Yea, Isaiah."

"I like that." she said, mimicking him, while taking a sip of water. He chuckled. His laughter carried on for a few more seconds and right when he was about to respond, another patron came in and sat at the bar. It was another woman. She was drenched from the rain and appeared to be trying to dry her phone with some of the napkins placed on the bar's counter. "One second," he told Essence.

Isaiah went over to the woman and asked what she'd like to drink. She replied, asking for a martini, requesting for him to hold the olive, and asked for a shot of vodka on the side. After fulfilling the woman's requests, Isaiah walked back over to Essence. She was holding her debit card in her hand, ready to pay for her drinks.

"You're leaving already sweetheart?" Isaiah asked.

"I am. Got to work in the morning. If I can inspire one child, then I've succeeded in life."

"You're a teacher?"

"Yes. I teach middle school English. Eventually I want to open up my own after school program for aspiring writers. I always say, if a child learns to read, they'll learn to write and eventually learn to properly communicate. I just want to guide them down the right path"

Isaiah smiled. He admired her. In such a short time he noticed the way her hair was imperfectly placed into a high bun, yet neat and appealing at the same time. The way her eyebrows raised when she was curious, and how she'd tilt her head slightly to the left when she smiled, and straighten her glasses, enticed him. Her brown eyes would squint when she giggled, and she'd rub her nose, adjusting her nose ring. Her skin was equivalent to toffee, and it was glowing, and mesmerizing. He was in awe of her beauty. Finding out she was an educator, made him appreciate her. "I'm glad I met you Essence. I enjoyed talking to you."

Essence handed Isaiah her debit card and said, "If you decide you want to talk to me again, I'll give you my number. I enjoyed talking to you as well."

"Ok, sweetheart. That sounds good to me." he slid Essence his phone so she could input her number. "I look forward to hearing from you Isaiah." He placed his phone back into his pocket, returned her debit card and watched as she walked to the exit.

The rain had slowed down and was mere sprinkles when she left Randy's. Her car was parked a block away from the bar, and right when she was about to unlock it, her phone started buzzing. She fumbled through all the miscellaneous things in her purse, trying to find it before it forwarded whoever was calling to voicemail. Barely picking up before the last ring, she nervously answered, "Hello?"

"I didn't want it to be too long before you heard from me."

Chapter 2

Essence and Isaiah spent hours on the phone that night. They talked about things that were so cliche' like their favorite colors. and ventured into deeper conversations about their families, politics, and even shared things about their children. Isaiah was tall, muscular, in shape, and had amazing skin. He was almost the perfect shade of caramel with a hint of honey and had beautiful brown eyes. His hair was cut short, and wavy, and his beard was clean and trimmed. The two diamond studded earrings he wore were the perfect accessory to his smile. He was gorgeous. He had a fourteen year old son from a previous relationship named Emmett. During the week, Emmett lived with Isaiah, and on weekends, and during the summer he visited his mom. Isaiah and Emmett's mom divorced when Emmett was eight.

Somehow Essence met Isaiah during a time when she was completely adamant about not getting into anymore fuckin relationships. The stress that came with them wasn't worth it. "I've always been the one carrying the weight. At least that's what it's always felt like," she told him. "Well, maybe I can carry some of it for you." He assured her. He went on talking about his dad, and how he was a musician, traveling from city to city, playing the piano for different artists. His dad had recorded four of his own solo piano concertos and was even nominated for an award for best original concerto.

"While he was working on his fifth, he got really sick. His heart was inflamed, because there was a lot of fluid surrounding it, preventing it from pumping properly. They called it pericarditis. He'd already gone into cardiac arrest before my mom found him in the basement at his piano."

"Wow, I'm sorry to hear that. That must have been gut wrenching for your mother. How old were you?"

"I was fourteen. But you know, my OG made sure I was good. My mom made shit happen. That's why I make sure I take care of her now. Whatever she needs, I'm there, for sure."

Essence smiled, occasionally twirling some of her hair around her finger. Her smile turned into a faint chuckle.

"What is it?" he asked.

"Nothing, just something my father said to me before he died that I thought about just now."

"Care to elaborate?"

Essence took a breath and responded, "He said, always pay attention to how a man treats his mother. That's going to be how he treats you. His mother is his first example of how a woman carries herself. She's his first teacher. So, pay attention to how he treats her. That'll tell you everything you need to know about how he'll love and take care of you."

"Sounds like your dad was a wise man."

"He was. He just couldn't stop drinking. He didn't know this, but I used to pour his beers out to try and stop him from drinking so much."

Isaiah laughed subtly. "He didn't notice?"

"Maybe. I don't really know. He'd just go buy more anyway. The one thing I remember about my dad, is how he'd have a forty ounce of Old English malt liquor on the kitchen table, while peeling potatoes, and The Munsters playing on the small tv that sat on top of the refrigerator. My mom would be seasoning whatever meat was for dinner, with a slightly frozen half drank Pepsi on the counter, and she'd be sliding and swaying in her slippers back and forth between the fridge and the stove. At some point, my dad would stop her in mid-stride, and motion for a kiss. She'd give him one and continue cooking. Those were good Sundays."

"Do you have any siblings?"

"An older brother. We're not close." she answered, immediately shutting down a follow up question.

"I have a younger sister. Only by a year though. She's an herbalist."

"An herbalist?"

Isaiah cackled. "She sells medicinal marijuana. I just call her an herbalist because it sounds better."

Essence laughed so hard.

The following weekend, Essence was running late to her therapy session with Dr. Reed. Dr. Reed had spent the last five years counseling Essence. It started with guiding her through her divorce and watching her spiral out of control abusing alcohol. The trauma truly became uncovered when Essence opened up about being sexually abused as a child, which in turn triggered conversations about her choices in men and the things she's allowed in her relationships. As of recently, they've been diving into Essence's relationship with her teenage daughters, Noa and Harper and her complicated relationship with her mother. Noa was sixteen, sassy, and sensitive. She loved art and painting. Anytime she showed her paintings, Essence would jokingly say, "Picasso who?" Noa was like night and day, and it showed in the ways she dressed, her random disassociation with people, her bubbly and energetic moods, and then, there were her episodes where she'd completely shut down for days at a time. Noa was diagnosed with major depressive disorder, and general anxiety disorder. Most days were good. She was calm, and pretty much what Essence believed to be a normal teenager. Harper was fourteen, feisty, and athletic. She was a star point guard on their high school's basketball team; being the only freshmen on the varsity team. Harper was resilient. She never let things bother her and found humor in almost everything. She and Noa were like ying and yang, two peas in a pod, close like white on rice, and all that other shit. Essence raised them to always protect each other, and never let anyone come between them, even their own mother. She wanted to break the cycle of toxicity in mother-daughter relationships, in her family and ensure her daughters didn't experience and have to heal from inadequacies they were never able to address with her. Essence was uncovering things about her past that in retrospect was causing her to actively unlearn and re-teach herself ideas and lessons that were instilled in her about love, parenting, and just overall womanhood.

Noa took it the hardest when Essence divorced their father Korey after five years of a verbally, emotionally, mentally, and abusive marriage. Noa was only eleven when Korey came home one day and packed all of his things. She and her sister watched as he threw different clothing items in his suitcase, his toiletries from the bathroom, shoes, his music equipment, and anything else he felt like was his. Korey thought he was going to be the next hottest producer out of Chicago, and apparently didn't realize he needed money to actually make money. Essence often referred to him as a "fuckin bum," when he came up in therapy. It's like the walls were slowly closing in on Essence, Noa and Harper, the moment Korey walked out the door. He bid the girls goodbye, Harper only nine at the time, and told them he loves them, and he'd still get them on the weekends.

Noa burst into tears, eloping to her bedroom and slammed the door. She screamed into her pillows and curled up underneath her blanket sobbing. Essence could hear her wailing through the walls, and all of a sudden the world began to move in slow motion for her. Harper appeared to slowly walk to the couch in the living room. Essence watched as she sat down and turned on the tv, flipping through cartoon channels. Essence asked Harper, "Are you ok?" but the words didn't seem to catch Harper's ears. It's as though Essence was speaking but there was no sound coming from her. The room fell silent, and all she could hear were the clicking of the buttons on the remote as Harper flipped through channels and the cries of Noa. Essence blacked out.

"Now that I think about it, I called my mother that night he left us, and you know what she said as I sobbed into the phone?" Essence asked.

"What?" Dr. Reed answered.

"She said," What are you crying for?"

"Hmmmmm." Dr. Reed said.

"Here I am, balling my fuckin eyes out because for the third time this nigga left us, only this time he's for sure not coming back. He's pretty much abandoned our daughters, essentially left me to pay all the bills, and you're asking me why am I crying? Be fuckin for real." Essence explained.

"Did your mom have a good relationship with your ex-husband?"

"My mother hated him. She didn't even smile during our wedding. She despised the way I loved him despite his shortcomings. She would always say, "Essence, you could've done so much better. He doesn't deserve you." In a small way, I think she was relieved when he left for the last time. And the most fucked up thing about all of it; that motherfucker was in a new relationship less than six weeks later. Fuckin bum. He even stopped getting the girls on the weekends." Essence replied.

"I don't want to deviate from the original topic Ms. Jackson. Motherhood. I'm curious about something." Dr. Reed said.

"What's that?"

"What's something you do differently with your daughters than your mom did with you?"

Essence began fidgeting with the ring she always wore on her left thumb, while thinking of an answer. She scanned Dr. Reed's office, appreciating the calm ambiance that filled the room. There was a humidifier that changed colors as the cool mist pushed through the nozzle. The walls were lilac, and there were picture frames of all of Dr. Reed's degrees and accomplishments, as well as a few frames that had inspirational quotes. One of them reads: *Do not go where the path may lead. Go instead where there is no path and leave a trail.* Essence favored that quote by Ralph Waldo Emerson the most. She tried to live by it.

"I apologize to them when I'm wrong." Essence finally said.

"Interesting. Do you feel like elaborating?"

"Well, I realize sometimes that I yell at my kids for things they do, before I even inquire about why they did it, or things that I may find annoying or irritating, they have no idea about. I've literally screamed at them out of my own frustrations with other people and things, without taking into consideration their feelings. For example, I get frustrated when my money is low, and I'm behind on bills, and one of the girls asks me to buy them something. Just a couple weeks ago, I yelled at Harper about asking me for new basketball shoes before her first playoff game. I yelled about how I didn't have the money, and it's not fair to me that I'm the only one financially supporting them. I screamed for her to call Korey and ask him. In hindsight, I knew he would give her a dumb ass excuse about why he couldn't get them. I shouldn't have done that to her. However, I become so angry that I'm doing it all alone, and I kick myself every now and again, because of the choices I made. I apologized to Harper for yelling about the shoes and tried to explain to her that my feelings about finances and their father shouldn't have clouded my emotions. I got her the shoes the next time I got paid.

"Has your mom ever apologized to you for anything?"

"Never. I don't believe I've ever heard my mother say she's sorry about anything to anyone."

"Do you believe there's anything your mother owes you an apology for?"

"Absolutely." Essence began to get teary eyed. She grabbed a tissue from the box on the table and wiped away a tear from the corner of her eye. "Absolutely." she repeated.

"Why don't we pick up right here next week. I want you to write down everything you believe your mother owes you an apology for, and why. And then we'll discuss. How does that sound?" Dr. Reed asked.

"Sounds good."

Chapter 3

Harper's first playoff game was about to begin, and Essence could see Noa waving her down from the bleachers to come sit. She had just finished parent-teacher conferences at her job and was racing to Harper's game. She made it just in time for the jump ball. Halfway through the second quarter, Essence got a phone call. She hesitated before answering. Noa noticed the name on her mom's phone, and said,

"You gonna answer that?"

Essence looked at her and said, "No. I'm watching the game."

A few minutes later, her phone beeped, and it was a text message that read: *Hey sweetheart, call me after the game. Just wanted to wish Harper good luck.*

"Whoever Isaiah is, he really wants to talk to you ma. Sweetheart huh?" she teased.

"Noa get out my phone." Essence laughed. "Mind your business."

"Mmm hmm." Noa giggled.

Essence texted Isaiah back. *Hey Isaiah, I'll call you tonight. Thank you for wishing her good luck.*

Isaiah: *You're welcome.*

At the start of the third quarter, Harper was leading her team in points and assists. She had the ball at the top of the key, set up an isolation play, passed the ball to an open teammate who shot a three pointer creating a ten point lead for their team. The crowd cheered and stomped on the bleachers. They were chanting "Jaguars! Jaguars! Jaguars!" For the entire quarter, Harper dominated, even getting two steals, and ten more points of her own. The crowd could hear Essence shouting, "That's mine! That's my child! Let's go Harper!"

There were twenty two seconds left in the fourth quarter, and the Jaguars were no longer hanging on to a lead. The game was tied at sixty eight points. The other team inbounded the ball, setting up their next play. Harper, defending the ball, smacks it right out of her opponents hands, gains control of it and drives down court. Her opponent catches up to her and tries to block Harper's shot, not realizing Harper was actually passing it to her teammate on the corner at the three point line. Harper's teammate shoots, and the crowd goes silent. Noa and Essence stood on their feet, both with their hands in the air hoping for the win. The seconds on the scoreboard reached zero while the ball was still midair. Harper closes her eyes and hears the "swish" of the ball impaling the net. The jaguars high fived each other and patted each other backs, jumping in excitement. "That's what I'm talking about!" Harper shouted. "Let's go!"

"Good game girls! Way to hoop! That's how you start the playoff season!" Coach Bennett cheered.

On the way home, Essence played Queen's "Bohemian Rhapsody" at a high volume because Harper loved to listen to it after every win. She said it regulated her after all the adrenaline from the game. Ironically, it's a song that slowly progresses into a more aggressive sound, before ending very melancholy. It became a tradition after she scored the game winning shot in her first game in seventh grade. If they ever lost a game, Essence drove home in silence, while Harper replayed the game in her mind, randomly verbally pointing out areas she needed to improve in.

As the song ended, Noa asked, "So, who's Isaiah?"

"Isaiah?" Harper said, confused.

"He's nobody I want to discuss right now," Essence replied, trying to sound natural.

"Why not?" Harper asked.

Essence laughed. "Now, when did this car ride become an interrogation room?"

"I saw you smile when you looked at the screen when he called." Noa said unamused. "He must be somebody." she added.

"He's just a guy I met. He wants to take me out Saturday. I haven't given him an answer yet."

"Are you going to go?" Harper asked.

"I think I am."

Noa didn't say anything. She just kept scrolling through her phone. Essence perceived Noa's silence as disapproval. She knew Noa struggled with abandonment issues, and occasionally acted out when seeking attention. Noa was thirteen the last time Essence tried to date. She started lashing out in school, and at home, and would accuse Essence of leaving like Korey did. When she was fourteen, she ran away from home and falsely accused Essence of physically abusing her, getting child services involved, only for tax dollars to be wasted on a dumb ass investigation. Noa was just upset that her phone was taken because she was failing English. When Noa was fifteen, she got her heart broken for the first time by a boy, a junior, who told her he loved her and would never hurt her. There was a video circulating of him fucking Noa's friend Bianca. Noa cried for weeks. She couldn't shake the blatant disregard for her feelings, and it began eating her alive. Her demeanor changed. It was like a light switch went off in her mind. One night, a couple weeks before Christmas, Essence walked in on sixteen year old Noa in the bathroom sitting on the edge of the tub. There was a blade in her right hand sliding vertically across her left wrist. Essence watched the first draw of blood seep through Noa's skin, and she screamed, "Noa stop! What are you doing!" She grabbed Noa's hand screaming for her to drop the razor blade. "Drop it Noa! Let it go! What's wrong?! What's wrong?!" Noa screamed in agony and the blade fell to the floor. Harper, overhearing all the noise, quickly called for an ambulance. Essence started grabbing tissue from the roll and applying loads of it to Noa's wrist. She cradled her, hysterically crying asking, "What's wrong?! Noa what happened?! Why did you do this?! Noa tell me!" Noa wailed, and her wailing turned into screams.

"Everybody leaves! Everybody leaves me! He left us! He left and he didn't give a fuck about me! I needed him! I hate him! You're gonna leave us too! It's just a matter of time! I hate you so much! He left us because of you! Because you just wouldn't stop being mad all the time! You were always so mad! He told me one time ya know! He told me you made him sad! He said he was going to leave! He told me! He said he was going to take me with him! That's why I said you were hitting me! So, I could live with him! I hate you both! I hate Bianca because she fucked my boyfriend after he said he would never hurt me! Everybody hurts me! I don't want to be here anymore!"

Essence was horrified at what she was hearing. She wept and held the tissue on Noa's wrist until while waiting for the ambulance to arrive. Noa tried her hardest to pull away from her mother, but Essence wouldn't budge. She just hugged her and cradled her tighter, apologizing. "I'm sorry he lied to you. I'm sorry Noa. I'm sorry he hurt you. I'm so sorry

Bianca hurt you. I'm sorry Noa. What can I do to make it better?" The pit of her stomach felt like someone was twisting and turning all of her internal organs. She was in instant pain. The room began spinning, and Essence just held on tighter. She noticed Harper standing at the threshold to the bathroom door, and could vaguely hear her saying, "Ma, they're on their way. Noa, they're coming. Ma, can you hear me?"

Essence was barely making eye contact with Harper. She'd grown dizzy but wouldn't let Noa go. She just held on. They all sat on the floor by the tub, waiting for the ambulance to arrive. Essence and Noa sobbed, as Harper assisted Essence in holding tissue on Noa's wounds. It was the loud sound of the ambulance outside of their apartment that startled Essence, snapping her back to reality. She didn't even give the paramedics a chance to come in and get Noa. Essence picked Noa up, carrying her in her arms, as though she had just been born. Maintaining compression on Noa's wrist, she hurriedly said, "Harper open the door."

One of the paramedics ran to Essence, extracting Noa from her mother's arms, and took her inside the ambulance.

Noa was hospitalized for seventeen days after that. After she was formally diagnosed, Essence sought therapy for Noa, and placed her in an art program, where she also received counseling every other weekend.

"He just wants to go bowling, that's all. And maybe have a couple drinks." Essence said, breaking the silence. "He's a nice guy." she added.

Harper looked back at Noa, who was stretched out in the backseat. Noa didn't take her eyes off her phone. "I hope you have fun." Harper said.

Chapter 4

Isaiah arrived on time to pick up Essence. He held the passenger car door open and complimented her as she sat down. "You look beautiful sweetheart." His car smelled like the little trees black ice scent, along with a touch of his cologne. It was clean and free of paper or food and had 90s r&b playing softly. Essence could hear Tyrese asking a woman to be his sweet lady. He was insisting he'd be there when she needed him, all she had to do was call. "You like this kind of music right?" he asked.

"I do. Something about the nineties I just can't let go." she replied, singing along with Tyrese.

Isaiah gazed at her, and before putting the car in drive, he grabbed her hand gently, holding on, and said, "You ready sweetheart?"

Essence chuckled. "I'm ready."

Isaiah took the scenic route, cruising down lake shore drive, playing Brandy's *Have You Ever*, and Dru Hill's *Never Make a Promise*. Just as they passed the Ferris wheel at the Pier, Boyz 2 Men's *I'll Make Love to You* came on and Essence turned the volume up.

"I'm sorry I didn't mean to touch your radio, but I love this song!" Essence explained.

"It's ok sweetheart. Turn it up as loud as you want." he replied.

She added more volume and sang along with the four man group about making love ever so gently and becoming one with each other after. She loved the idea of a man professing his love to a woman and explicitly telling her how he'd love her and how he'd satisfy her. She loved the words and the images they created.

"This is the greatest love song I've ever heard!" Essence exclaimed. "It's so beautifully arranged, and I just feel every word, and the music is just powerful. I just love it." she continued.

room and showed Kameron Sr. He became livid and instructed Kameron to say nothing until Savannah got home.

"So, what happened when your mother got home?"

"Well, when I found out that my diary was missing, I ran to my dad and told him."

"What did he say?"

"He said he already knew it was missing and that he had it. He said he was waiting for my mother to get home so she could see what I thought of my family. So, I just went into my room, afraid of how the evening was going to go."

"How did that make you feel?"

"I felt betrayed. I felt betrayed by my father and my brother."

"What did your mother say after she read it?"

"She called me into the living room, where she sat with my father, and Kameron. She told me to stand. Then she started reading through the pages."

Essence recalled how their living room had off-white painted walls, and a cream and light brown couch. There was a mantle where a fireplace that couldn't be lit sat beneath it. On top of the mantle were pictures of their family, and some of Savannah's friends and their families. On the opposite side of the living room, was their TV and a long black marble coffee table, that sat on top of a tan, black and white patterned rug. There was a door in the far corner of the living room that led to a balcony. Sometimes, depending on the weather, Kameron Sr. would leave the door cracked open to let fresh air in.

Essence stood there. Her heart was beating so fast as she stared back at all of their eyes looking at her. The room felt small, and she felt even smaller in it. Kameron sat there with a frown that embodied hatred for Essence. Their dad, with a can of Old English, took a sip, cut his eyes at Essence, then shook his head slowly and looked away. Savannah was still flipping through pages of the diary. The sound of her house keys unnerved Essence as they dangled from her finger while she flipped through the pages. Savannah hadn't even taken her coat off before she dove into her daughter's deepest thoughts. The three of them sat on the couch, with Kameron in the middle. Savannah and Kameron Sr. kept eyeing each other as she flipped through more pages. The agony of watching her mother read her diary, some of the content aloud, ripped a hole into her heart. Essence's body grew numb after feeling like somebody was stabbing her with pins all over. She would shift her focus from her mom, to Kameron, to her dad, and then back to her mom. Her knees felt like they were going to collapse if her mom turned one more page. Just when Savannah was about to read aloud another page, Essence screamed, "STOP! Stop it!"

"Stop what?! Stop reading about how you really feel about us?!" Savannah yelled.

"You think I don't like you? After everything I've done for you?! Is that what you really think? Because I'm always at work, you think I don't like you? Talking about you wanna stab us? What is it that I don't know about you, Essence? Since I don't know you, why don't you tell me about yourself!"

"Mom, that's not what I meant!"

"Then what the fuck did you mean Essence? You calling your dad an alcoholic and saying Kameron should be in hell and you wish he wasn't here! What the fuck did anybody do to you?!"

"Mom! That's not what I me…"

"So, I'm an alcoholic huh? I drink too much. What fuckin bill do you pay? Who in the fuck are you to tell me I drink too much?"

"Dad.. I.."

"No! No, no, no! You don't get to cry now Essence! You wrote these things about us! I told you to write down your deepest feelings, not talk shit about us! If I ever believed you had three sixes in your head, it's right now! How dare you say these things?! Tell me! Why is your brother so nasty to you? Why is he trifling and disgusting and all these other things you say? What the fuck is so bad about your brother, who makes sure you get to school and home, cooks for you, takes you to the park, and helps you with your homework? Huh?! Tell me!"

Essence got dizzy. Her stomach sank to her knees, and her head started pounding. She could hear the faint sound of Kameron sniffling in the background, after Savannah yelled. He appeared to wipe away tears after hearing the things Essence was writing about him. She felt sick to her stomach. The nerve of him. Kameron looked at Essence with disdain as Savannah yelled. His face was telling Essence not to say a word. His eyes were dark and guilty. Kameron Sr. kept sipping his beer as Savannah went on. He would cosign the things Savannah was saying with a subtle "Mmm hmm," or "Exactly," showing his solidarity with her.

Essence stared at Kameron again before she spoke. When she tried, only cries came out. "Mom!" she cried. "You said I could write whatever was on my mind and my deepest thoughts and I did! Now I'm in trouble for it! Mom, please!" she begged her.

"I'm so fucking disappointed in you." Kameron Sr. said angrily.

"Mom!" she cried. "Please!"

For no more than a few seconds, Essence and Savannah made eye contact. Her mother's eyes were angry, and dismayed. Essence could barely see through the puddles of tears in her eyes as she pleaded with her mother for her diary.

"Apologize to him." Savannah said. "Apologize to your brother."

Essence wiped her face. Her sadness immediately became rage. "Apologize?!"

"Yes. Apologize. He didn't deserve that."

Essence shot Kameron with an evil look. She was furious. She couldn't believe her mother demanded she apologize to her brother. "I won't." She protested.

"Oh, you won't?" Savannah fired back. She then grabbed a few pages of the diary and ripped them out.

"Mom! Stop! Please!"

Savannah ripped more pages out. "Apologize!"

"Mom! Please! Stop it!" Essence wept as her mother ripped more pages from her diary.

"I'm sorry!" she yelled. "I'm sorry! Please Stop!"

Savannah tossed the diary to the side, with some of the ripped pages falling to the floor. "Now clean this shit up. You're on punishment until I say otherwise."

Essence was wiping tears from her face as Dr. Reed poured her a glass of water. Having to relive moments that trigger pain and sorrow was extremely overwhelming for her. Essence didn't hate her family. She despised the fact that as a child she wasn't heard no matter how loudly she tried to speak, even if the right words didn't come out. She felt like her whole family betrayed her in different ways, and somehow still found a way to fault her.

"How did your mother make you feel at that moment, when she ripped your pages?"

"She betrayed me. I felt like I had no one to stand with in my own family. I never understood why she didn't scold my brother and my dad for reading my diary in the first place. And then she told me to fucking apologize for what I wrote! She was supposed to protect me and my privacy. She was supposed to read between the lines. Instead, she berated me and belittled me, and showed me in that moment, even her own words meant nothing."

"Do you talk to your brother at all?"

"I only see him when I show up to family holiday events. I don't talk to him outside of that."

"Has he ever apologized for the things he did to you?"

"We've never talked about it. I buried it deep."

"When did it stop?"

"When my dad died. It was about six months after the diary incident. He died of cirrhosis of the liver."

"Has Kameron tried to reach out to you outside of family events?"

"He's tried, but I don't respond. I figure if I keep my distance, it'll go away, and I can live my life peacefully."

"You understand that's not how healing from trauma works right?"

"I understand it's been working for me all these years. I have a career, my own place, a car, and I take care of my kids. I pay all my bills myself, and I don't ask nobody for shit. I'd say I'm doing pretty well."

"You also drink heavily, don't sleep much, cry a lot, don't know how to regulate your emotions, and haven't dealt with the things from your past that keep you up late at night. These are all responses to unhealed trauma. I'm only saying these things because you need to learn how to address problems head-on without being overly emotional about them, so you can find a solution. Your solution cannot always be a shot of tequila, casual sex, late nights, and shutting down when you're upset. You need to work your way through your trauma Essence. You cannot leave it sitting somewhere idly while you go on living your life, and then wonder why you're crying in the middle of a malt liquor aisle in a grocery store because you pass a can of Old English. Or you flinch at the sexual advances of a man, because you oddly remember at that moment your brother's molesting hand. Or you yell at your daughters for expressing themselves even if it hurts you, because that's what your mother did, instead of treating them like they also have feelings. Essence, you are not your trauma."

"She always made me feel like I couldn't come to her with my secrets, or like I had to learn things on my own because the world didn't owe me shit. There were times she was nice, and Christmases were joyful, and the Sunday dinners were memorable. However, my mother wasn't affectionate with me. I can't tell you the last time she hugged me. She's always been harder on me than Kameron and I don't know why. She called me stupid when I got pregnant with Noa, because I was young, and Korey wasn't shit. But when Kameron got a bitch pregnant, my mother couldn't wait to see if his baby would have our father's hazel brown eyes. I resent her for things that she may believe are trivial, like not telling me I looked beautiful on my wedding day, or asking me a month after my father died, why did I love him more than her. I still haven't answered that question. Now that I'm an adult, we barely talk. I see her when I drop off her medicine or she needs to go to the store. I've distanced myself recently. I realized even in her old age, she's still the same person. Entitled, unapologetic, self-righteous, and narcissistic. I honestly don't think she'll ever be able to love me the way I need to be loved by my mother. That's why I allow Noa and Harper to respectfully express to me when they think I'm wrong about something or they were hurt by something I said or did to them, and I make sure I apologize. I let them know their words, feelings, and desires matter, as long as they aren't harmful to anyone else."

"Eventually, you are going to have to address your mom and brother, for your own healing."

"But what if they don't want to hear it? Or what if they deny my experiences?"

"Denial is the enemy of acceptance. If your family decides to negate your experiences, then there's nothing you can physically do about it. They have to live with their decisions. On the contrary, when you accept that your experiences happened, whatever they may have been, and find a way through that pain, then and only then will you begin to know what genuine healing is."

"Thanks Dr. Reed. I'll work on it."

"I'll see you in two weeks, Ms. Jackson."

Chapter 11

Essence rushed home, carefully switching lanes through traffic, so she could make it home and get ready for her date with Isaiah. Traffic wasn't heavy, but Essence hated being late for anything. She was extremely anal about being on time. It was a sign of respect for her. When she got home, she greeted Noa and Harper, who were watching TV on the couch.

"Hey, how was school?"

"Fine!" They both replied.

"Y'all eat something for dinner?"

"Yup!"

"I'm going out with Isaiah tonight, so..."

"We know mom!" they laughed.

"I don't know how late we'll be out, so don't wait up for me."

Noa and Harper looked at each other and giggled. "I'm sure she'll be spending the night with Isaiah tonight." Noa whispered. Harper laughed.

"I'm going to take a shower." Essence told them.

"Ok!"

Noa continued scrolling through her phone, while Harper started flipping through channels again. "Are you ok with mom dating again?" Harper asked.

"I'm ok with it."

"You sure? You remember how you reacted last time."

"And that was last time. I'm better now Harp. Chill."

"I'm just saying, it scared me last time. You scared me."

Noa put her phone down and looked at Harper with sorrow and understanding in her eyes. "Harper, I'm sorry. I am. I know I probably never said that to you, but I am really sorry. I was going through something really dark, and I hated Korey for how he did us, and Anthony and Bianca. It was just a lot."

"I watched mom hold you like a baby, and she was screaming, and you were screaming too. There was blood and… and…" she began to cry.

"Harper, I'm so sorry. Come here." Noa hugged Harper, holding on to her and rocking her from side to side. Harper cried into her sister's arms, pulling her in closer. They wept and embraced each other for several minutes. "I'm sorry Harper. I'm ok now. I'm not gonna scare you like that again. I promise. I got you. I'm sorry Harp."

"You promise Noa? I thought I wasn't gonna see you again."

"I promise Harp. I'm not going anywhere."

About thirty minutes later, Essence came back to the living room and asked, "Do I look like I'm dressed comfortably?"

They giggled. "I mean you definitely look like you're going to chill and eat slices of pizza all night," Harper laughed.

Essence was dressed in black leggings, with a fitted lime green t-shirt that had a picture of palm trees on it with the word Miami in gold bold print. She finished her outfit off with green sneakers, and a ponytail.

"Ma, take off that t-shirt and put on a tank top. It's still a date," Noa teased. "That's a shirt you wear to the laundromat or when you visit someone at the hospital to brighten their mood."

"Damn Noa, tell me how you really feel." she laughed.

"I'm just saying, he said dress comfortably, not like you're about to barbecue."

Harper cackled. "Not barbecue!"

"Ma, it's April now, and it's warmer out. Just keep the leggings but change into that fuchsia pink tank top you just bought; you know the one that you said makes your breast look perky. He'll like that. Also, put on some white sneakers, and carry your white zip up hoodie in case it gets chilly. That'll look cute together. Lastly, take that ponytail out. You are not going to church. Let your hair down and keep a hair tie on your wrist in case you have to put your hair back up. But if you have to put it back up, make sure it's in a messy bun. I heard men like that on women who wear glasses. Apparently it makes them look sexy."

Essence was in utter disbelief at Noa's constructive criticism. "Sexy huh?" she smirked. She went back to her room to change clothes and came back wearing exactly what Noa suggested. "Now you look sexy, and like you're ready for fun." Harper smiled.

The doorbell rang exactly at eight o'clock. "Ok, that must be him." she said casually. In secret, Essence melted at the thought of a man who understood time sensitivity. When she opened the door, Isaiah stood there dressed in black from head to toe. He wore a fitted black t-shirt that showed off the cuts in his biceps and triceps, and you could see some of his abs poking through the shirt. His jogging pants were from Nike and were loose enough for his third arm to have some breathing room. He wore black Timberlands that weren't fully laced up, and black socks. His silver chain that hung just below his collarbone was the perfect accessory to Essence's secret fetish. A man dressed in all black did something to her spirit. She loved how it made them look mysterious, yet sexy and gentleman-like at the same time. A man in all black gave her that millisecond of a numbing feeling women feel in their pelvis when they recall a sexual encounter or moment with their lover that satisfied them. Isaiah stood there exuding confidence, charisma, charm, and poise.

"What's up sweetheart." He kissed her and continued, "Fuchsia looks good on you." Essence turned back to Noa and winked. "Thank you." She leaned into whisper something in his ear, "You remembered that I love a man in all black?"

"I remember everything you tell me. I listen to you, even when you think I'm not."

She smirked, and grabbed his hand, bidding Noa and Harper goodbye. "Come on, we should go."

Halfway through the drive Essence asked, "So, where are we going tonight?"

"I wanted to do something fun, but soothing and therapeutic at the same time. I know you're in therapy, so I wanted to take you somewhere that may help you decompress."

She smiled with somewhat of a confused look on her face. "Fun, yet soothing and therapeutic?"

"Yea. I made reservations for a candle making class, followed by a dinner, where we'll light our candles over grilled salmon, cilantro and lime rice, asparagus, and red wine. I rented the place out for you."

Essence was in awe. She gazed at him as he drove with his left hand on the steering wheel, cruising through traffic, and his right hand holding on to hers. She saw fireworks when she looked at him. A man she met at a bar, renting out a place just for them to make candles and have dinner was such a romantic thing for him to do, she thought.

"How does that sound sweetheart?"

"Sounds like you know exactly how to help me decompress. That sounds amazing."

He gently raised her hand to his lips and kissed it, as he pulled into the parking lot of Drea's Candles and Cocktails. After putting the car into park, he turned to her and said, "You deserve to be treated softly, spoken to calmly, and loved correctly."

If they weren't already at Drea's Candles and Cocktails, Essence would have pulled his dick right out of his pants and swallowed every inch he was blessed with. She was turned on by how settling and comforting his voice was, and how he made her feel safe and secure with him.

"That means a lot to me. More than you know."

"You mean a lot to me, sweetheart," he replied.

Drea's Candles and Cocktails was beautiful when they walked in. There was dim lighting and the tables that would normally fill the room were moved, leaving only one medium sized circular table and two chairs. Usually, there would be one side of the establishment where people made their candles, and on the other side, they'd eat dinner and light their candles. Next to the table was a cart filled with supplies for candle making. There were different colors of candle wax, oil fragrances, a small boiler, wicks, candle dye, a pitcher, containers, and a stirring tool. There was a white nylon cloth that draped over the table. On top were two aprons and latex gloves. There was classical music playing at a low volume in the background from Mozart, Beethoven, and Bach that catered to the peaceful ambiance.

"Good evening Isaiah and Essence. My name is Zara and I'll be your host this evening." Zara was dark skinned, like the color of chocolate. The dim lighting bouncing off her skin was mesmerizing. She smelled of cocoa butter and cinnamon and wore blue jean overalls over a spaghetti strapped red halter top, and black sneakers that were stained with candle wax residue. Her lips were plump, covered in clear lip gloss, any man would love to kiss, and she wore a gold hoop nose ring in her right nostril. Her hair was thick, full, and curly and styled in two long French braids that dangled past her shoulders. Her fingernails were short and polished with a nude color, and she wore a ring on or middle finger that was shaped like the sun. There was a small tattoo on the left side of her neck of a heart monitor beeping into the shape of a heart, that read: *Life Life and Be Free.*

"Tonight, you are going to make candles that represent peace, longevity, patience, and love. There are many different wax colors to choose from for your candle, and I also have scented fragrances for you to choose from for your candle. First, I will show you how to make your candle, and how to properly use the tools that I've provided for you. I will then leave you two to have some privacy and enjoy each other's company. The chef will be preparing your meal while you create your candles. I've placed a bottle of Merlot on ice for you all if you'd like a glass while you make your candles and wait for your meal."

Zara proceeded to guide Isaiah and Essence through the candle making process, teaching them how to use the boiler and the wicks and use the candle dye. They laughed as Essence squirmed at some of the oil smells, and toasted with a glass of wine when they finally got the hang of mixing the wax.

"Ok, it looks like you both are set and ready to start making your candles. Remember, peace, longevity, patience, and love. Chef will begin making your food now. Enjoy your evening.

As Zara walked away, Isaiah slowly pulled Essence's chair closer to his and kissed her cheek. "I couldn't wait for her to give us some privacy." he chuckled.

"I really appreciate what you've done tonight. This is beautiful."

"You deserve it sweetheart. Now, what fragrance did you pick for your candle?"

"I like earthy smells, so I went with this one. It's called 'rainforest'."

Isaiah smelled it. "Smells nice. Not too strong. I like it."

"Which one did you pick?"

"I'm a guy who loves the smell of citrus. It reminds me of a spring morning, after it rains the night before. So, I chose the one called, 'orange paradise'."

Essence smelled the fragrance and moaned. "Damn, that smells good. Mmm. I love that. That was a great choice."

"Thank you."

Isaiah watched her out of the corner of his eye, concentrating on molding her wax. She chose a dark Greek color for her candle and a white wick. He gazed as she poured the 'rainforest' fragrance oil and green dye into her mixture, stirring with ease. She wanted the color of the candle to match the smell that would eventually come from it. As she finished pouring her wax into the container to cool, Isaiah began to add his mixture. He decided to make his candle a yellow-orange color to match the citrus smell. He stirred his colors and fragrance oil together, heated the wax, and poured his creation into his container to let it cool.

As they waited on their meal, Isaiah fixed them another glass of wine. "Are you enjoying yourself?"

"I am." she blushed, taking a sip,

"I'm glad you are. I hope that eased some of your stress."

"It did. It was comforting, and relaxing. I felt like all I could focus on at that moment was my candle. I needed that after the session I had today."

"Therapy?"

"Yea, Dr. Reed has me unlocking all this trauma from my relationship with my mother, and it gets really frustrating and emotional sometimes."

"I'm sorry to hear that. Is therapy helping?"

"It's helping. She holds me accountable for my healing process. She told me the only way to heal from my trauma is to accept that it happened, and address my issues accordingly, despite who negates them. She said, "denial is the enemy of acceptance."

"Interesting. Relationships with our parents are hard. I resented my father for a while for dying so suddenly, and my mom spent years being upset with me for going away to college. She felt like I left her too. Even though she took such good care of me even after he died, she started to become obsessed with me not leaving her. It drew a wedge between us for a few years because as soon as I graduated high school, I left and went off to school.. It was hard trying to get her to understand that I needed to go out and be a man. I wasn't leaving her. I just grew up."

"I understand. Is your relationship better with her now?"

"Oh, yea! That's my OG. We solid."

"That's beautiful. Maybe I'll be able to say that about my mom one day."

"You will sweetheart. It all takes time. And even if you don't, you'll be healed from whatever it is that's weighing you down."

"You know how to say all the right things don't you?" she smiled.

He kissed her forehead, and then her lips. "I say what's necessary. And if it sounds right, then I've done well."

The chef came out with their dinner. It was served on white glassware that had tiny decorative flowers painted around the edges. You could see the steam coming from the grilled salmon that was placed on top of the cilantro lime rice. The dark lines in the salmon from being pressed on the grill sizzled. There were four spears of asparagus on top of the salmon, seasoned and buttered. There was also a lemon and honey sauce drizzled over the entire meal. It looked like a piece of art. The chef topped their wine glasses off, lit their candles for them and wished them an enjoyable meal.

After they ate, drank, and continued on with deep conversation, they gathered their candles and left. Isaiah drove to his apartment, so they could finish the evening with dessert, conversation, and more wine. When he opened the door to his apartment, there was a bouquet of yellow and white lilies on the coffee table. Essence told him one day that those were her favorite. Next to the bouquet was a fresh bowl of strawberries, and chocolate syrup. Her favorite dessert. There was a bottle of Merlot, chilled, and two wine glasses. Her favorite wine. There were rose petals spread across the floor, leading the way to this gorgeous display Isaiah had set up. His apartment smelled exactly how he described his candle. Like citrus from an orange after a rainy day. His curtains were slightly opened, letting in the evening light, and in the corner of his living room, next to the mounted sixty inch TV, was a standing lamp set to low lighting. His couch was sectioned off, with the long end facing the tv, and the shorter end facing the entry to the apartment. There was gray carpeting that appeared freshly shampooed that covered his living room floor. Hanging on the wall on each side of his TV were photos. One photo was of Muhammad Ali, and the other was Malcolm X. Isaiah believed they both embodied the true nature of what it meant to fight, just in different ways. Essence couldn't believe the way Isaiah planned the evening. It was the most romantic thing she'd ever experienced.

"Dessert?" he asked.

Essence smiled at him with alluring eyes, and began stepping out of her sneakers, and unzipping her hoodie. Isaiah closed the door behind him, helping her remove her sleeves from her arms. He rubbed her shoulders and stepped out of his boots. He kissed her, impaling her mouth with his tongue, pausing to subtly lick her top lip, and then intensely kissing her again. Essence held him by his belt buckle, walking towards the couch. Before they sat, she unbuckled him, and leaned her forehead on his chest. His cologne entered her nasal passage, and she bit her lip while sliding her hand into his pants grabbing on to every inch. She massaged him and he groaned and throbbed in her hand. His pubic hairs were soft, not prickly, and moisturized, and the skin on his dick was smooth, free of random ridges or bumps. He was clean and smelled amazing.

"Essence," he moaned.

"Sit down." she demanded, removing her hand from him, and sliding his pants down.

He sat on the couch and locked eyes with her as she lowered herself to her knees. She took his dick into her hand and kissed the tip of it before sliding her tongue from the bottom of it back to the tip, before submerging it into her warm, saliva filled mouth. He took her hair on both sides into his hands and assisted her with motion as she went up and down sucking and massaging his shaft with her tongue. She rubbed his testicles with one hand and rubbed his dick up and down with the other while she sucked.

"Baby," he moaned. "Sweetheart."

She kept going, faster and more controlled. She could feel him swelling and gripping her hair tighter. The sounds that came from her sucking excited him. His moans excited her, so she moaned with him. "Baby," he cried. "That's it. Don't move. Stay there Essence. Baby, oh my God. Fuck!"

It was warm and thick, but not like peanut butter. More like honey but watered down a little. It splashed into her throat, and she kept going until there was nothing left for him to give. He softened, and his body sank into the couch. Isaiah took a sigh of relief and helped her up. Essence took her middle finger wiping the corner of her mouth, and started to pour a glass of wine, but he stopped her.

"Hold on. It's my turn."

He laid her down on the couch, removed her clothes from her body piece by piece, and sucked each nipple while stimulating her clitoris with his thumb. She squirmed as her insides warmed. Isaiah took the bottle of chocolate syrup and poured a small amount over her starting at the center of her neck. He drizzled it over her breast, the middle of her stomach, her inner thighs, and finally her clitoris. He licked and sucked everywhere except her vagina until there was no more chocolate. Before he began to devour her, he kissed her in the mouth, leaving chocolate residue on her lips and whispered in her ear, "Can I taste it?"

She whimpered. "Yes. Please."

"I love when you beg."

He went down and seductively traced her vaginal lining and opening with the tip of his tongue, before moving forward with her clitoris. He circled it, licking up syrup, and kissing it in between swallowing the syrup. Once all the chocolate was gone, he inserted two fingers into her, caressed her g-spot, and continued sucking on her clitoris until she exploded. As soon as he felt her gushing into his mouth, he got up and inserted himself into her thrusting and moaning. He whispered her name, and she said his back. Isaiah gripped her thighs and pulled her hair. He made love to her. "Are you ok sweetheart?" he whispered. "I'm ok baby. I'm ok." He stroked her slowly, and then sped up, slowing down again and then speeding up again. "You feel it?"

"I feel it Isaiah!" she cried.

"You love it don't you?"

"I love it!"

"You feel so good inside. I feel you coming baby. Come for me Essence."

Her body felt like an inferno. His voice in her ear made her mouth water as she held on tight. Her thighs began to stiffen, and her heart began to race.

"Isaiah," she moaned. "Isaiah.."

She felt a wave of emotions come over her as he thrusted again, squeezing her thigh as it hung over his shoulder. His next stroke was so perfect, it caused him to loudly moan her name, "Essence!"

She moaned back in satisfaction, as tears rolled down the sides of her face, "Isaiah! I'm about to…"

"Me too!"

Their bodies became one as they orgasmed together. She kissed his shoulders as he laid on top of her. They could still feel each other throbbing as their bodies slowly returned to normal. He kissed her chin and then her lips before sitting up. Essence sat up next to him, both fully nude.

"Dessert?" he laughed, picking up a strawberry. Essence laughed and took a bite. She poured a glass of wine for Isaiah and then herself. She noticed she still had the hair tie on her wrist from earlier, so she decided to put her hair up, to let her shoulders and back breathe from all the sweating. She put her hair into a quick messy bun, and found her glasses that fell on the floor, and put them on. Isaiah picked up his glass, and tapped hers with his and they took a sip. He stared at her silently, as she sat naked eating strawberries and sipping wine.

"I like the hair bun. It's sexy."

Chapter 12

Sunday evening, Noa got a text message from Anthony that read: *Noa can we please talk?* As much as she wanted to answer, she ignored the message. She remembered her therapist telling her that she should never lend her energy to someone who hurt her. It's fine to forgive them, but forgiveness should not equate to a revolving door. Thirty minutes later, another message from Anthony popped up on her phone. *I'm really sorry for what I did. I broke up with Bianca. I miss you.* Noa rolled her eyes and continued working on her painting for the art competition. It was six weeks away, and she wanted it to be perfect. All she could think about was the competition. If she won, she would be awarded five thousand dollars in prize money, a ten thousand dollar scholarship to any art school in the country, and an all-expenses paid trip to Disney World. The competition was sponsored by an art gallery called, The Painting Palace, that showcased paintings from all over the world. Every year, the gallery organized an art competition offering young artists in high school the opportunity to gain recognition, providing a platform to help launch their future careers in the art world. There was nothing that was going to get in the way of Noa winning that competition.

The next morning at school, Anthony was waiting by Noa's locker for her. She was walking with Harper who pointed him out saying, "Look what the cat dragged over to your locker." Noa looked up and instantly became annoyed at him standing there with a sad face, like someone ran over his dog. "You want me to walk over there with you?" Harper asked. "Nah, I think I'll be ok." Harper could sense Noa was trying to play it cool. However, she could tell in Noa's tone of voice, and the way she looked down at her shoes when she answered, she wasn't going to be ok. "I'll walk with you anyway."

"What do you want Anthony? I need to get in my locker."

"Can we please talk?"

"No. There's nothing to talk about. Now can you move so I can get in my locker?"

"Noa, I messaged you last night saying I'm sorry."

"I know. I got them. I was busy."

"I broke up with Bianca. I should have never been with her. I didn't mean to hurt…"

"Didn't she say get away from her locker?" Harper interrupted.

Anthony looked puzzled. He adjusted the strap to his book bag on his shoulder, and sighed. His attempt to ignore Harper didn't work because when he tried to speak again, Noa interrupted him again and said, "You heard my sister. You need to move."

"Noa please just talk to me," he pleaded.

"Move."

Harper side eyed him as he stepped between them moving away from the locker. "Thanks Harp." Noa said. "Girl, I got you. That nigga's a clown. Noa, I'm sorry, please," Harper laughed, mocking him. Both girls busted into laughter as Noa finally got her locker open to grab her first period books. "I got chemistry first period, Mr. Maxwell's class. Fuck my life." Noa groaned. "Alright, I'll see you later then. Chin up Picasso." Harper was about to walk away, when all of a sudden she heard someone yell Noa's name. She turned to see Bianca coming straight for Noa, and Harper jumped in between them.

"Who you feeling like today Bianca?!" Harper said, asserting herself, and dropping her book bag. "Mike, Muhammad, Roy Jones Jr. perhaps?" she suggested.

"I got it Harp."

"I saw you talking to Anthony. What the fuck was that about? You're the reason he broke up with me bitch?"

"He broke up with your nasty ass because he wanted to you fucking waste of nut. You probably burned him with your dirty ass. Now, watch out. I got chemistry."

Students began to gather around all of the commotion, as Bianca walked closer to Noa. "Don't take another step Bianca, I'm telling you." Harper warned.

"Harp, you got the game Thursday. Don't."

"And you got the art competition. Walk away."

"Anthony just fucked me last night! What the fuck did you say to him to make him break up with me after he left?"

"Hmmm, maybe something smelled fishy, and he just couldn't take it anymore Bianca. I don't know, and I don't give a fuck. Now, move!"

"Or, maybe because he found out you tried to commit suicide before Christmas, and felt so sorry for you, and just had to make you feel better. Yea, I told him."

Noa became irate, dropping her book bag from her shoulders, yelling, and screaming about how she was about to fuck Bianca up. Other students started instigating, cheering Noa and Bianca on. No one knew about why Noa missed those weeks of school back in December, except

Noa's mom and sister, Principal Malone, Noa's therapist and counselors, and Bianca. Bianca only knew because her mom was a nurse that worked at the hospital Noa was admitted to. Unfortunately, now, the whole junior class knew. Bianca hit Noa so far below the belt, it enraged Harper. In the midst of Noa berating Bianca for mentioning her suicide attempt in front of everyone, Harper had already taken a swing at her, closed fist, right in the eye. "Harper!" Noa screamed. "Noa, go to class! I got it!" Noa picked up her things, and started in the opposite direction, trying to squeeze between students that formed a crowd. Bianca stumbled back after she was hit, but Harper didn't stop. She punched her again, this time in her nose. Blood began to pour from Bianca's nostrils. "I told you not to fuck with Noa. I told you when we found out you fucked him, and I told you after I saw you at the hospital, but you didn't listen!" She punched her in the mouth, splitting the skin on her top lip. Bianca fell to the floor and Harper jumped on top of her punching her as hard as she could. Bianca tried covering her face and was screaming for Harper to stop. Harper kept striking her, and even slapped her a couple times. "I told you don't fuck with Noa!" Harper was about to punch her again, and that's when a security guard snatched her up from Bianca and pulled her away. He carried Harper as far away from the fight as he could before standing her back on her feet. Bianca laid there bludgeoned. Her face leaked of blood, and she wailed in agony. Harper was sent to the principal's office. "Get to class! "yelled the security officer.

"Ms. Jackson, I hear you were in a fight. What happened?" Principal Malone asked. He was stern and didn't take shit from anyone. He wore a suit every day, and always had a cup of coffee. Principal Malone was in his late fifties, brown skinned, bald, and had a salt and pepper beard. He was a no nonsense type of guy.

"She was about to hit my sister and I didn't want her to mess up her chances of being in the art competition."

"Why didn't you walk away Harper. You're the captain of the basketball team and you're only a freshman. That's a huge accomplishment. Why would you want to mess that up?"

Harper began to fidget with her fingers and took a deep breath. She didn't want to answer.

"Harper, why would you mess up your chances of being on the team? You know there's a no fighting rule."

"So, I'm off the team?"

"I didn't say that. That's up to Coach Hill."

"She mentioned in front of everyone how Noa tried to commit suicide before Christmas. Noa was about to relapse and fight her, and I had to protect her." she cried. As tears were falling, Harper continued.

"Noa has had a rough time. You know with the divorce and her mental health. I can't let people bully her. She goes through enough. That was a dark time for us, and Bianca should have kept her mouth shut."

Principal Malone exhaled a sigh of sadness. "I'm sorry for everything your family has been through Harper. But I can't condone fighting." He said, handing her a piece of tissue. "I have to speak with Coach Hill, and we'll decide what to do from here. In the meantime, I have to call your mom, and she'll have to come pick you up. I can't allow you to go back to class."

When Essence arrived to pick up Harper, she found out why Harper was fighting and demanded to speak with the principal and Coach Hill. Essence stormed through the hallways looking for the principal's office. The floors of the school were tile, and white. The walls were light blue, and the students' lockers were small and gray, with one locker above another one. The school smelled of lunchroom pizza, and tater tots. The doors to each classroom were brown with the classroom number in bold stickers attached to the door. The bell rang for the end of first period, and students rushed the halls traveling to their next class. Essence eventually pushed through the stampede of students and made it to the principal's office.

"Good morning Ms. Jackson. How are you?"

"I'm fine. How are you?"

"I'm well. I was informed that Harper got into a fight today with another student, due to some harsh things that were said about Noa." Principal Malone said.

"So, why is my child the only one in trouble and not Bianca?"

"Well, Ms. Jackson Harper took the first swing."

"Because Bianca approached Noa as if she was going to hit her, and Harper said she stepped in to protect her sister. Are students not reprimanded for provoking students into a fight? Do you expect your students to always walk away when someone is inciting violence against them? Are we not living in the real world?"

"Ms. Jackson…"

"I'm not saying that violence is the answer, but sometimes, violence becomes the only answer."

"If I may interrupt…" Coach Hill said. "I am in no way saying that I believe what Harper did was ok. However, I'm aware of some things that your family has been through because Harper confides in me. Ms. Jackson, I empathize with you and your daughters, which is why I am not going to remove Harper from the team. However, I do believe that she should be held accountable for her behavior, as well as Bianca."

"Thank you Coach." Harper said, taking a sigh of relief.

"You will serve an in-school suspension tomorrow, along with Bianca. You will also run twenty five suicides at practice after school tomorrow. Finally at some point, before Thursday's game, you will apologize to Bianca."

"Apologize?!"

"Yes. As team captain, you need to set an example. I know you're only a freshman, and you're carrying the weight of an entire team. I know you can do it though. You've shown me all year. Harper, there are people who look up to you even though you're younger than them. Be the example. Be an inspiration."

"Ok, Coach."

"Thank you Coach Hill. And thank you Principal Malone." Essence said. Harper carried out her in-school suspension the next day and ran her suicides in practice like Coach Hill told her. She also apologized to Bianca the morning of Thursday's final playoff game. She had a bruised eye and a slightly swollen lip, and flinched when Harper

approached her. "I'm just here to say I'm sorry." Harper assured her.

Bianca didn't reply. She just continued walking to class with her head

down. That night, Harper led her team to the all-city championship with

twenty six points, eight assists, and six steals. All she had to do now was

prepare for the championship.

Chapter 13

Essence stared at her phone, contemplating calling her mother and

Kameron to confront them about the past. It was a Saturday, and the

April rain subsided as the sun struggled to peek between the 5pm gray

clouds. She was sitting on her bed, picking at her nails, while she glared

at Savannah's number. At times, she would switch to Kameron's number

and stare at that one. She was stumped on who she should call first, or if

she should just do a three-way phone call. The last time she talked to

Kameron was during Christmas two years ago. Savannah had summoned

them to her house for the holidays, and Kameron struggled trying to

make small talk with Essence. To keep the peace with her mom, Essence would show up to a gathering, stay a couple hours, and then she'd leave. That way, Savannah could never say that Essence never came around.

She finally got up the nerve to call her mom and Kameron on a three-way phone call, after she took a shot of tequila. She kept a bottle in between her nightstand and her bed, and any time she felt overwhelmed, she would pour a shot, sometimes a glass. If the days were really stressful and depressing, she'd finish the bottle. It got to the point where the clerk at the neighborhood liquor store knew what she wanted whenever she came to purchase alcohol. "Fifth of Jose' Cuervo Gold?" he'd say. Essence had been in denial that she was a borderline functioning alcoholic. She believed that since she maintained a comfortable home, had a career, took care of her kids, showed up to their events, and kept her bills paid, how much she drank was irrelevant. Suddenly her body felt numb, and she got teary-eyed as she waited for Savannah to answer.

"Hello."

"Hey ma. How are you?"

"I'm good. Same shit different day."

Savannah was finally retired from scouting models. Her career went downhill when Catwalk was bought out by a bigger agency. Some of her relationships with clients and colleagues were severed because

Savannah always thought things should be her way or no way at all. She became hard to work with and labeled as difficult. After her retirement she appeared unfulfilled and unhappy. Everything was negative with her. Her pessimism drained Essence. No matter what the situation was, Savannah was going to find something wrong."

"I was calling because I wanted to talk to you and Kameron about something and I think we should all discuss it together."

"Talk about what?"

Essence hesitated. "Well, there were just some things that I needed to talk to you about to get some understanding."

"Understanding about what? Why you always speaking in riddles?"

"I'm not speaking in riddles ma. I'm just telling you why I called."

"So, what does Kameron have to do with this conversation?"

"I think it would just be better if I called him on a three-way. Hold on."

Essence clicked over to her other line and called Kameron. She took a deep breath, and wiped away another tear that was sliding down her cheek.

"Essence?"

"Yea, Kam, it's me. Hold on, let me merge mom in."

"Hello? Can you both hear me?" Essence asked.

"Yea," they both replied.

"Essence what is this about?"

"Ma, you know I've been in therapy for a while now, and there are some things I need to do in order to heal from my past and move forward so I can have a more comfortable and enjoyable future."

"Okay, so what does that have to do with me and Kameron?"

"Before dad died, I wanted to tell him something, but I never got the chance to. So, I just buried it."

"Ok..."

"Ma, you were at work a lot, and dad would be sleeping or at the store, and stuff would happen."

"Essence what the fuck are you talking about?" Kameron interrupted.

"Kameron, you know what I'm talking about."

"No, I don't know what you're talking about. Why the fuck did you call me with this shit?"

"Essence, what is this about?"

"Ma…." Essence began to cry. She sniffled and fumbled through her words. "Kameron would do stuff to me." she cried.

"Do what?" Savannah asked, confused.

"Ma, nobody protected me!"

"Protect you from what?!"

"Kameron!"

"Essence, you're not making any sense. Why would I have to protect you from your brother?"

"Because he used to touch me! He would rub on me and do nasty things that a brother and sister shouldn't do! And he knows it! And you ripped up my diary when I tried to tell y'all! But I got in trouble! He would kiss me and touch my private parts and show me his!"

"That's bullshit Essence and you know it! I never touched you!"

"That day when dad fucked him up for beating my ass is one of the days it was happening! I just didn't tell the whole story because he said we would both get in trouble!"

"Essence what do you mean he used to touch you?" Savannah asked.

"Ma, I just told you! I don't want to go into details! He molested me!"

"I didn't touch you!"

"Are you sure this happened? It sounds like a one-sided story to me. He's saying he didn't and you're saying he did."

"Am I sure this happened? One-sided story? It's not a fucking story mom! It happened! And if you weren't at work all the time and dad wasn't drunk, you would have noticed what the fuck what going on! You didn't find it weird that I didn't want to wear skirts and dresses or night gowns! You didn't notice the pissy sheets, and me not wanting to be in the dark?!"

"Essence, you were a tomboy! I knew that's why you didn't like the dresses!"

"It wasn't because I was a tomboy mom! I was trying to make it harder for him to touch me at night or when you would be gone! I thought all boys were like that, so I didn't want to wear them to school either! But you thought I was being difficult! You never asked me questions. You just always assumed."

"Essence, I told you if there was anything you ever wanted to talk about, you could have talked to me. I had to work! And if he's saying he didn't do it, and you're saying he did, then what exactly am I supposed to believe!"

"You're supposed to believe me! I'm your daughter!"

"And he's my son!"

The phone call went silent. Essence was taken aback by her mother's response. She couldn't believe that even when she was being that vulnerable, opening up about her sexual abuse and trauma, Savannah still couldn't understand that her daughter was crying out for her. She was so lost in her own thoughts and denial, that she was blind to what was literally right in her face. The fact that Kameron was denying everything was no shock to Essence though. She expected that. It was the harsh reality that Savannah wasn't going to understand. She still wasn't protecting Essence and shielding her from the pain. She continued to show the inability to give Essence the comfort and care she desperately needed.

"Think about it mom. Really think about it. Would you lie about something like this? Something this serious?"

"I'm not saying you're lying. I'm just saying there are two sides to every story."

"But it's not a story! Stop calling it that! You both are deflecting, diminishing, and negating my experiences and trauma and what I went through in that house! For God sakes, you told me you thought I had three sixes in my head! You called me stupid because I didn't want to get baptized because I didn't understand the bible. You never supported my dreams! You thought I wanted to be a chef because I liked making homemade cheeseburgers and fries. You didn't listen to me when I asked you to put me in gymnastics, or figure skating, or that I wanted to be a teacher! You didn't listen when I begged you to take me with you out of town! You didn't listen when I would purposely fall asleep in you and dad's room, so I wouldn't have to go in mine! You didn't listen when I came to you because my vagina was itchy, and it was red and irritated, and you just blamed me saying it's because I don't wipe myself correctly! You didn't listen! You didn't pay attention! You never paid attention to me! You probably never even liked me! You said how could I be so stupid when I got pregnant with Noa. She tried to commit suicide last year and I couldn't even call you to tell you, because I knew you wouldn't make me feel better! When Korey left us, you asked me why I was crying about it, as if my husband leaving me with two kids doesn't warrant sadness. You…"

"Essence he was a fucking loser. He was a bum!"

"Even now, you still don't get it! It's not about Korey! It's about me! It's about what happened to me, and you still don't give a fuck."

"Look, I raised you and Kameron the best way I could. I did my best. When Kameron Sr. died, half of me died with him."

"What about before he died ma? It was happening then."

"I did what I was supposed to as a mother. I took care of you."

"Yea, financially! When's the last time you remember hugging me ma? When was the last time you asked me how I was doing? When was the last time you were affectionate towards me? You were never affectionate. But I guess you're right. You took care of me."

"I need to get back to work," Korey said sarcastically. "I don't know why you called me with this shit Essence. You definitely need therapy, and I hope you get the help you need. Love you ma."

"Kameron, fuck you." Essence sneered. "Fuck you and that dirty ass horse you rode in on. You know exactly what the fuck you did to me."

Kameron hung up his line and left Essence and Savannah to continue with the conversation.

"You know what ma, I thought this would be helpful, but all it did was set me back. The things I endured in that house did happen. And whether you believe me or not is up to you. You were supposed to notice the signs. You were supposed to see me, even when I acted invisible. You didn't even ask him if it was true, and that is heartbreaking in itself. You just took his word for it that it wasn't. When are you ever going to see me?"

"If you don't think I care about you, that's something you have to figure out. I'm not going to spend time trying to convince you that I care or that I love you."

"When has love ever been enough ma?"

Essence ended the call and poured a shot of tequila. She sat there on her bed for the next few hours, drinking and sobbing. There were tissues balled up on her bed from wiping her nose and her tears. She poured another shot. The bottle was halfway empty when she got a phone call.

"Hello?"

"Hey sweetheart. I miss you. How's your Saturday going?"

Essence instantly broke down, consumed by a torrent of cries, like an ocean in a thunderstorm.

"Baby, what happened? What's wrong?" he asked worriedly.

"She didn't believe me! He lied. I tried to tell her! And she.. she.."

"Who Essence?"

"My mother!" she wept.

"Sweetheart, what do you need from me? What can I do to help?" Isaiah was concerned and taken aback by her level of emotion. He'd never seen her like this.

Each tear that fell seemed to steal her words, making it harder for her to speak. Isaiah listened to her sobs, as they came in waves, each one making it harder for her to collect herself. He gave her time to get it out.

"Baby I'm here. Whatever you need. I can come over and sit with you if you want."

She forced herself to calm, summoning all her will to find the words to respond to him. "Can you?" she cried.

"I'm on my way."

When Isaiah arrived, Noa opened the door surprised to see him. "Hey Isaiah. What are you doing here?"

"You're mom needed me. She asked me to come over."

"Oh, she's in her room. Everything ok?"

"Yea, everything is ok. She's just having a rough day." he replied.

Isaiah went to find Essence in her room, sitting on the floor by the bed, with the half-drunk bottle of Jose' Cuervo. He closed the door and sat beside her, removing the bottle from her hand. Essence was overwhelmed. Her eyes were red and puffy from crying and her nose needed to be wiped again. She pulled her knees to her chest and laid her head on Isaiah's shoulder. He snatched a piece of Kleenex from the box on the floor and gently wiped her nose. "You can tell me. What happened?" Essence went on to explain the conversation with her mother and Kameron. She dove into her past and gave detail on her traumatic experiences, sobbing in between explanations. Isaiah listened intently, his heart aching as he wiped away his own tears, realizing the depth of the agony she endured as a child. His compassion for her ran deeply. Isaiah pulled her in close, silently promising an unwavering vow that he'd never leave her side and would always be there in her time of need.

"Sweetheart, I'm sorry that you had to experience all of that. You deserved better. I can't begin to fathom the anguish and distress those horrible and heinous acts created inside of you. Baby, I'm so sorry. You are beautiful and intelligent, and you are raising two amazing girls. You are powerful beyond your own imagination. The weight of what you've been through makes it all the more important for you to have someone who catches you when you feel like you're about to fall. Let me catch you. You don't have to be in pain forever."

His eyes softened as he gazed at her, brushing her hair back with his fingers. His voice was serene as he promised her everything would be okay.

"Will you stay with me tonight?"

"Of course, sweetheart. I'll stay as long as you like." He helped her to her feet and then into the bed. There was a knock on the door, and it was Harper. "You ok ma? We heard you crying."

"I'm ok now Harp."

"Ok." Harper looked at Isaiah for confirmation. He nodded his head, assuring her that Essence was fine.

"Hey babe, I was thinking about ordering some pizza. Maybe we can all watch a movie or something to cheer you up."

"Pizza sounds great!" Harper said, jumping into the bed. "Noa! Isaiah is ordering pizza! Come watch a movie with us!"

Noa came to their mom's room and laid across the foot of the bed with Harper. Isaiah ordered the pizza and climbed into the bed with Essence, cuddling her into his arms. In that moment, she felt the safest she'd ever been in her entire life. They turned on a comedy movie about two black guys, one a scammer and one a banker, who got falsely accused of killing a man, after going to purchase illegal alcohol during prohibition, and got sent to prison for life.

Chapter 14

Harper's first high school championship game was moments away, and she was a bundle of nerves. Anxiety crawled underneath her skin, and she was on edge, battling to hold herself together. They were set to play the Hornets who's point guard averaged twenty eight points a game, nine assist, five steals, and at least one block. She was number nineteen and her name was Staci, but her team nicknamed her Bullet because of how fast she was on the court. She stood maybe an inch taller than Harper and wore her hair in French braids that were straight to the back. There was a rumor circulating that Staci was bragging about how she was going to break Harper's ankles on the court and score thirty points. One thing about Harper though, the players never intimidated her. It was always the pressure of the game and winning that drove her anxiety through the roof. Harper exuded confidence on the court. There was no way another girl was going to come onto their home court and break anybody's ankles, nor score thirty points.

Harper stretched her hamstrings during warm-ups and gazed at the crowd. The gym room at Southside High had no empty seats, and the chatter of all those watching the high school game of the year boosted Harper's adrenaline. She spotted her mom, Noa, Isaiah and Emmett in the stands and waved. Essence blew her a kiss and mouthed the words, "good luck." Noa stood up with a sign she decorated that said *Go Harper! #3 The Clutch!* Harper smiled as Noa swayed side to side waving the sign. She showed Noa gratitude for the sign, overcome with emotion for her big sister's support. They gave each other air high fives, as the buzzer went off for the start of the game.

Both teams huddled up with their coaches, to prepare for the game with strategizing and motivation. "Alright girls! You made it this far! This is what you have worked all year for. I am proud of you all and

I want you to go out there and show those stingless Hornets how we ball at Southside High! Are you ready?!"

"Yes coach!"

"Captain! You know what to do!"

Harper began:

"When our backs are against the wall, what do we do?!

"Fight!"

"Any time one of us falls, what do we do?!"

"Get back up!"

"Are they tougher?!"

"No, we are!"

"Are they faster?!"

"No, we are!"

"Do we fail?!"

"No, we win!"

"Say it again!"

"We win!"

"One more time, Jaguars! What do we do?!

"We win!"

"Jaguars on three! One.. Two.. Three!"

"Jaguars!"

Harper drove down court passing the ball to a forward, who passed to their center who was right under the net. She scored a layup right at the buzzer for halftime, bringing their score just six points shy of tying the game. The score was 47-41, and Harper was exhausted. Staci was putting pressure on her every time she came down court, making it hard for her to score. Harper was stagnant with only eight points at the half.

"Harper what's happening out there! Where's your head at?! You're letting her control your game, your movements. She's not better than you. Stop letting her think she is! You got a secret weapon Harper. Use it!"

"I'm sorry Coach!"

"I don't need you to be sorry. I need you to win! All of you. Hustle for it! You didn't come this far to let them take it from you did you?!"

"No!"

"Are you gonna leave here without that trophy?!"

"No Coach!"

"What do you do when your back is against the wall Jaguars?!"

"We fight!"

"So go out there and prove to them why you all deserve this!"

"Yes Coach!"

"Hustle up!"

As the Jaguars made their way back to the court, the immense energy that came from the crowd cheering them on lit a fire under Harper. The center inbounded Harper the ball and she flew down the court, dribbling with her right, then her left, and between her legs. Staci stayed on her, refusing to let her get past. Harper passed the ball and spun around Staci to get to her spot underneath the basket. Harper's teammate passed the ball back to her, and just as she got ready to go up for the layup with her right hand, she switched it to her left as soon as Staci tried to block it. The ball rolled off her fingertips into the net, and the crowd erupted into cheers and applause.

"That's what I'm talking about Harper! Use that left! Use that left! That's money!" Coach Hill shouted. Staci was in disbelief. Harper constantly switched her stance as she dribbled and shot the ball, showing equal skill between both hands. She was crushing the Hornets shot after shot. Staci could barely keep up with which way Harper was going to go.

She threw dime passes to her teammates adding more assists to her stats, and managed to attempt and succeed at stealing the ball three times that quarter. Harper ended the third quarter with twenty two points, seven assists, and three steals. She was so excited for the fourth quarter; she could barely maintain her composure.

"Ok ladies. This is it. The last quarter. Give it all you got and leave everything on the floor tonight. Remember, I'm proud of you and I believe in all of you. Now go out there and bring us a championship! Jaguars on three! One.. two.. three..!"

"Jaguars!"

There were four minutes left on the clock and the game was tied at seventy points. Harper drove inside the paint for a layup and got fouled hard by Staci. Harper fell to the floor and the crowd gasped. Essence and Noa stood up searching through the players, waiting for Harper to get up. The referee blew his whistle calling for a foul, as Harper rose to her feet, adjusting her basketball shorts and eyeing Staci. Essence cheered. "Yea, Harper! Always get back up! That's my daughter right there!"

Harper approached the free throw line, and the crowd went silent. She dribbled the ball and practiced two air free throws with her right hand, and then did the same thing with her left. When she practiced the air free throws with her left hand, she winked at Staci with certainty and determination in her eyes, confident she'd make her shots. She shot the first one and it went in, all net.

"Woo! Go Harper!" That voice was different coming from the crowd. It was a man's voice, but it wasn't Isaiah's voice nor Emmett's. Harper scanned the crowd looking for whose voice that was. It sounded familiar to her. She dribbled the ball once more and the referee motioned for her to shoot. Harper looked back into the crowd before she took the shot and finally made eye contact with the person cheering her on. She was startled and dropped the ball.

"You ok?" the referee asked, handing her the ball back. Harper didn't respond. She just kept looking in the crowd at the familiar voice. She shifted her eyes to Essence and made eye contact. She then shifted her focus back to the mysterious voice, and Essence followed Harper's gaze.

"What the fuck?!" Essence shrieked as she looked over and saw Korey in the crowd. "How the fuck did he know about her game?" she thought. Noa followed Harper's gaze and stood up.

"Noa, let it go." Essence whispered.

"He shouldn't be here. Why is he here? Tell him to leave!"

"I can't tell him to leave a public event Noa."

Isaiah looked into the crowd and noticed Korey a few rows down, and behind them. "Y'all ok?" he asked. The concern in his tone was evident.

"Yea, we good. Let's just watch Harper finish the game."

"Hey! Number 3, shoot your free throw!" The referee demanded. Harper snapped out of it and made the shot. "Woo! That's my girl!" Korey shouted. Noa looked at him with fury in her eyes.

"He got some nerve ma. He's going to distract her."

"Noa, ignore him. I know it's hard seeing him. But right now, we are here for Harper. Don't ruin it for her. If she's not fazed by his presence, don't become so consumed with it either."

Something about Korey randomly showing up to the game, evoked anger in Harper. She was fuming, but she took it out on the court. Three minutes remained and Harper was dominating. Staci was on her, defending the ball, and Harper dribbled it to her left, then between her legs and back into her right hand. She dribbled the ball behind her back attempting a spin, only to go in the other direction, tripping Staci up, causing her to stumble over her own feet. Harper pulled up with a three point shot and brought their lead up to five points. She sprinted for the ball if the Hornets missed a shot, trying to get the rebound. In Harper's mind, she was the only one on the court. She tuned out the noise of the crowd as the clock wound down. The Hornets managed to tie the game again with only twenty seconds left on the clock. The crowd was on their feet as Harper came down court with the ball. They chanted Harper's name. "Harper! Harper! Harper!" She passed the ball to the center who was right underneath the basket. She went for the layup and missed, grabbing her own rebound, and finding Harper in her favorite spot on the court. The right corner. She swiftly passed the ball to Harper, who was setting her feet. Three… two… Harper shot the ball. One…

She closed her eyes after releasing the ball. All she could hear was silence. She felt like the gymnasium went dark and she was alone. Harper heard the ball fall through the net and when she opened them, she was being rushed by her teammates and Coach Hill. "That's how you do it Clutch!! That's how you win a championship ladies!" Essence, Noa, Isaiah and Emmett came down the stands and onto the basketball court to celebrate and congratulate Harper. They were high fiving her and shouting great job, when Korey walked up to Harper mid-celebration.

Before he could speak, Noa stepped in between them. "You need to leave. You have no right to be here."

"I'm just here to cheer Harper on, Noa."

"And exactly where were you the last five years Korey!"

"Noa, calm down." Harper said.

"I am calm. You are not going to ruin her moment with this random display of joy and praise for her accomplishment. You should be ashamed of yourself!"

"Harper, I heard some people talking at the barbershop about number 3 on the Jaguars and found out they were talking about you. I just wanted to see you play."

"Well, now you've seen her. Please leave us alone right now Korey." Essence interrupted.

"Look, I'm talking to my daughter, not you Essence!" Korey fired back.

"Aye man, watch how you talk to my woman. Seems like you feeling tough today, why don't you raise your voice at me bruh." Isaiah said.

"Man, watch out." Korey responded. "If that's what you call a woman, you might want to get your eyes checked."

Isaiah approached Korey closely, not even a few inches apart, his voice measured, but laced with an untamed, dangerous tone. "If you enjoy eating with a fork and not through a straw, I suggest you get the fuck up outta here."

Korey sized Isaiah up and chuckled. "Is that a threat? Was that supposed to scare me?"

"Dad, would you just leave? I really don't want to see you right now. Just go." Harper scolded him. Her words pierced him. There was nothing left for him to say. He left without so much as a goodbye to Noa and Harper.

"Thanks, Noa. I thought you were about to hit him." Harper laughed. "I was! Talking to mama like that."

"Good game Clutch!" Emmett said, lightening the mood. "Thanks."

"Pizza anyone?" Isaiah asked. "I'm driving."

"Nah, I think I deserve a steak tonight," Harper said, holding up her MVP award. "Just make sure you play Bohemian Rhapsody on the way.

Chapter 15

It was the Friday before Mother's Day, and Dr. Reed requested that Essence come in early to her therapy session. She was ending her sessions early because she was leaving for the Bahamas for Mother's Day weekend. She didn't want to leave without talking to Harper first, to discuss the conversation with her mother and brother. So, Harper took a half day at work, and came in around one o'clock. "I hope I'm not inconveniencing you in any way Harper."

"No, it's fine Dr. Reed."

"So, how have things been the last couple of weeks?"

"Things have been okay. Harper won her championship game and was awarded MVP. Noa has her art competition coming up soon in a couple weeks. She's been really stressed about that. She wants her piece to be perfect."

"I'm sure she'll do well. She has amazing talent. Both of your girls do. You should be proud."

"I am. I'm proud of them every day." she smiled.

"And Isaiah? How are things with him?"

Essence blushed. "Isaiah is…. like a breath of fresh air after emerging from deep waters. He calms me. He held me after I cried into his arms about my mother and Kameron. He stayed with me that night, ordered pizza and watched movies with me and the girls."

"That was sweet of him. Is it getting serious?"

"I think so. We spend a lot of time together, and our children have already met. I think about him all the time, even when I should be focused on other things. I always want to know what he's doing, or if he's eaten throughout the day. I want to know how his job is going, installing electrical wiring at the building that used to be Jon's Furniture Store. Sometimes he texts me sweet things while I'm at work, or he'll send me sexy voice messages, to make me smile. He's nice to me. He makes me feel safe and secure with him. He doesn't make me wonder if I should trust him. He actually leads. I haven't had to lift a finger since I met him."

"That's really good Essence. I'm glad you're actively finding love again. You deserve it."

Essence wasn't opposed to continuing a discussion about Isaiah. She could talk about him all day if Dr. Reed let her. "I know you want to know how things went with my mom and Kameron. I honestly don't really know where to begin."

"Why don't you begin with how they made you feel after confronting them."

She took a minute to think before she responded. Dr. Reed's office was silent. Essence could hear the ticking sound of the second hand on the wall clock that sat above Dr. Reed's desk. She observed the second hand sweep its way around the clock, shifting from 1:15 to 1:16.

"Essence?"

She focused her attention back on Dr. Reed. "I felt like a ticking time bomb. I felt like I was going to explode. Kameron denied everything, and my mom didn't even give me the benefit of the doubt. She defended her parenting, and she even defended Kameron against my accusations. Unfortunately, the only person she didn't defend was me. She never even asked him if he did it. She just took his word for it that he didn't."

"Do you think your mom carries any guilt for not realizing what was happening at home when she wasn't present?"

"I don't know. I don't know how she could feel guilty about something she acts like she doesn't even believe happened."

"Mothers are complicated Essence. I'm sure your daughters think you are harsh with them sometimes without understanding why."

"That may be true. The difference between my mother and I, is that I would never condition my children to believe that one child means more than the other. That's how I felt my entire life growing up. Like my mother thought Kameron was more important than me."

"Why do you feel like Kameron was more important?"

"It doesn't help that my mom told me she got pregnant with me while she was on birth control. She said I was an oops baby. Sometimes I think she only wanted one child and resents me for being born."

"Do you think you're being a little too hard on your mother?"

"No. I'm being honest about how I feel about my mother. I love her very much. Sometimes, I just don't believe she's ever going to give me the love that I needed from her. And that is what hurts the most."

Dr. Reed surveyed Essence's disposition. She was twisting her ring on her thumb and shaking her leg back and forth after crossing it over the other. She was looking down, her face unveiling a sadness that words couldn't explain. Her hair was in a neat ponytail, and she wore little silver hoop earrings that she would tug at every now and again when she spoke out of frustration. She wore a navy blue blazer that matched her slacks, with a white silk blouse underneath, and dark brown flat soled shoes. Essence looked defeated.

"What is your fondest memory of your mother Essence? What's the one moment you will always remember you and your mother sharing?"

"That's easy." Essence replied. "Her wedding day. She was beautiful. She radiated an unparalleled elegance and beauty, like a royal queen, and I was her princess. We quietly prepared for the wedding in our dressing room. I was her flower girl. Her white dress, enriched with delicate pearls along the lining, was nothing short of majestic. The sheer fabric near her collarbone revealed just a hint of skin, enumerating the gracefulness of the dress. The gown's length flowed effortlessly to the floor, and its train resembled something straight out of a fairytale. She wore white pumps, with sparkling diamond-studded heels and a diamond necklace that was illuminating. I was in awe of her. She told me so many times that day that I was beautiful while hugging me and kissing my cheeks. We took a lot of pictures, and she twirled me around in my little white ball gown, calling me a princess. I cried watching my parents say "I do" to each other and light their unity candles. She danced with me a few times at the reception. Sometimes my feet would be on top of hers as

I emulated her dance movements. I don't remember dancing with her much after that. I don't remember her ever being that affectionate with me again"

"How do you perceive the other good times throughout your childhood and teenage years?"

"Most of them I look at like, those were good times because my mom was in a good mood. Other times when we would go to a hotel for the weekend and spend time swimming, watching movies and eating takeout are moments I cherish as well."

"Do you think your mother was a bad mom?"

"No. I believe my mother tried to do what she was supposed to do as a parent. However, I strongly believe she neglected me emotionally. The times where it was essential that she discerned my body language, my dissociation and isolated mood, to be able to determine the level of emotional care I needed, is where I feel the most disconnected with her."

"Do you think you'd ever be able to say that to your mother?"

"I don't think I'll put myself in another situation where I'm yearning for something she probably isn't mentally and emotionally equipped to give me. That's why I just wrote her a letter. Whatever she deduces from the words I wrote is for her to deal with, not me."

"A letter? Do you have it with you?"

"It's in my email. I can pull it up if you want to hear it."

"I'd like that."

Dear mom,

I want to start off by saying, I don't blame you for the things I experienced growing up with Kameron. To be completely transparent, it did happen. I wouldn't lie about something like that. The unfortunate fact is that because it happened, it left a stain on my idea of safety, protection, and family. You taught us to protect each other and love one another no matter what. How do you expect me to love my brother after he defiled me and took away my innocence, only to deny it and insult me with needing to continue therapy. I thought you would have at least given me the benefit of the doubt and believed for just one second, that I was telling the truth. It brought me back to the day you all read my diary. That's the moment when I understood what it meant to not trust people. You all betrayed me. You read my most private thoughts, and even in the midst of reading them, you nor my father questioned anything. I will never understand why. Ever since I can remember, I felt like I was only visible to you when I made the perfect grades, or it was time to visit your family, and you wanted to show everyone how beautiful your daughter was compared to their children. I don't remember getting many hugs growing up, but I do remember being screamed at for asking you to buy me black underwear. You said I was trying to be fast, and who did I plan on wearing those underwear for. I was thirteen. I only wanted them for when I was on my period because I didn't like staining the other panties. I didn't even know women wore black underwear with the intention of sleeping with a man. I remember you calling me stupid for getting pregnant with Noa, and not even smiling at my wedding. You didn't even accompany us to lunch after. You never cared for Korey and that's fine. But it didn't help with all the other shit I was dealing with in my marriage, listening to you tell me all the time how much of a bad decision I made marrying him. You didn't talk to me. You talked at me. And some of the advice you did try to extend, came across as very judgmental. You were harsh and unaffectionate. Telling me you thought I had three sixes in my head is heartbreaking. Why would you say that to your daughter? You thought I was the devil, and all I wanted was to be seen by you. I got good grades. I didn't get in trouble at school. I didn't steal. I didn't fight. I did my chores. I wasn't a perfect child, but assuming my constant attitude was because I was standoffish and essentially just had an attitude problem, is insane to me. Did you ever think that maybe, just maybe, I was going through something? No. You didn't. And that hurts. When I was talking to you and Kameron, I noticed the sincerity in your voice when you said, "And he's my son!" I don't hear that same sincerity when you speak to me. For a long time, I admired you. I aspired to achieve your level of success. I wanted to be like you. But it just seemed like you didn't even like me. Even now as an adult, the only time I talk to you is when I reach out to you. Don't you wonder how we're doing or if we need anything? I don't feel like your child. I just feel like someone you know. I want you to understand that I do love you. I will always love you. I understand now that some love has to be distributed from a distance. I'm different with my daughters. I apologize to them when I'm wrong. I allow them to express themselves and give them room to make mistakes without condemning them. I hug them all the time and tell them I love them and that they matter. I'm trying to break the cycle. Harper won MVP at her championship basketball game and Noa is entering an art competition. I met a man too. He's incredible. I want you to know that we're doing ok. And I want you to know that at least I know you tried. Happy Mother's Day. Love E.

Dr. Reed was wiping tears from her eyes. She was moved by the letter Essence wrote her mother. She gathered herself, dabbing the corners of her eyes with a tissue to dry her lingering tears. "That was something Essence. I think you said what needed to be said and it shows growth. Loving someone from a distance even if it is a parent is necessary sometimes for your own mental health. Every day you must put your mental health first because you have two children who are looking at you every day like a superhero. And Essence, I want you to know, you are truly a superwoman."

"Thank you Dr. Reed."

"You're welcome. When are you going to give her the letter?"

"I mailed it to her days ago. I'm sure she'll be receiving it soon."

"I really hope you enjoy your Mother's Day Essence."

"Thank you Dr. Reed. I hope you have fun in the Bahamas."

Chapter 16

The day of the art competition at The Painting Palace finally arrived. Noa was a nervous wreck. She hadn't slept much the night before because she was trying to add finishing touches to her piece. The woman in her painting was stunning, even though she was sad. The woman's background were hues of a deep royal blue accented with gold. It was shadowed by hues of purple and black, which brought out the gold color. The woman's eyes were reservoirs of suppressed memories, their depth housing secrets only the most curious minds could envision. The pearls around her neck were defined, hugging her neck, and her brown skin was radiant. The canvas was 24x36 inches in length and width, and Noa made sure to fill up the entire canvas with paint. Her nerves didn't take away from her confidence in her artwork. She had never entered her art into a competition, so she was nothing but hopeful about the outcome. Noa dressed herself in a black tea-length dress, with a V-neck collar. Her hair was styled in a sleek high bun, with mini curls flowing down the sides of her face. She wore ruby studded earrings and a gold necklace with a ruby pendant that rested on her neck, adding to her elegance. She topped her wardrobe off with wedged black heels that didn't overcompensate her overall look.

"Hey Picasso! Are you excited for your big day?" Essence asked.

"I think I am. I'm nervous, but I'm ready. Do you think I have a chance at winning?"

"Girl, I've already packed your bag to Disney World." she teased. "Of course, I believe you have a chance to win. You are a phenomenal painter Noa. I think you held a paint brush correctly before a toothbrush."

Noa cackled. "Thanks ma. I appreciate it."

"No problem. Come here."

Essence embraced Noa tightly. "I'm so fuckin proud of you Noa. You've come a long way. I know you're going to win."

"Thank you."

"Now, let's go. You wanna get there early so you can set up."

Isaiah and Emmett met Essence, Noa and Harper at The Painting Palace. Isaiah and Emmett both wore black tuxedos, with a bow tie and black dress shoes. "You both look handsome." Essence said, greeting Isaiah with a kiss. "You smell good." He whispered. He gazed at her, keeping his seductive thoughts a secret. To him, Essence was the most beautiful woman in the room.

"Hey Harper. You look beautiful today. Red looks good on you."
Emmett said. Harper was dressed in a red flowing sundress that was just
above her knees. She accessorized with a silver bracelet, necklace, and
diamond studded earrings. Her hair was straightened, just past her
shoulders, with a small portion of it pulled behind her right ear, revealing
her diamond earring.

"Thanks Emmett. You don't look so bad yourself."

"Do you want to walk around and look at some art while we wait
for the competition to start?"

"Yea, that's cool with me." Harper agreed.

Essence and Isaiah walked with Noa to the area of the gallery
where all the contestants were setting up their artwork. They were
instructed to leave their paintings covered until the start of the
competition. There was a table specifically for each contestant, with their
name, and the name of the piece they were showcasing. The card on
Noa's table read: *Noa Jackson, 16. "He Said He Wouldn't Hurt Me."*

"Wow look at my name! It looks so important, and so
professional!" Noa said excitedly. "It does." Essence agreed. "I'm gonna

stay here and finish setting up. I don't want to walk away from my painting. You guys go look around. I'll be fine."

The Painting Palace had cream colored concrete walls that displayed a plethora of artwork. There were paintings of families, cities, animals, food, patterns of colors, and playful scenes like little black girls jumping double dutch, or a mom straightening her daughter's hair with a hot comb. There were tall, maroon, floor to ceiling poles that separated the different sections of the gallery. There was a section for abstract art, one for urban art, and a contemporary section, as well as others. All of these sections portrayed oil paintings, pastels, watercolor paintings, acrylic, and even spray paintings. The floors of the gallery were jet black with a glittery coating that made them appear to glisten. The lights were bright in the places where art was showcased and dimmed in other areas where people mingled away from the art. There were also several women and men dressed in black khakis and white buttoned down shirts, walking around the gallery serving glasses of champagne to the guests.

Essence and Isaiah were strolling the gallery and admiring the artwork, when Isaiah said, "Now that we're away from the kids, I guess I can say, you look sexy as fuck in that dress. I had to control myself when I saw you."

Essence was flushed with warmth and happiness by his words. Her off-the-shoulder dark blue cocktail dress accentuated her figure and fell slightly below her knees. Her silver chandelier earrings dangled, nearly touching her shoulders but not quite, and a silver necklace with a diamond pendant completed her accessories. She pulled her hair back into a low bun that flaunted her facial features, causing Isaiah to randomly plant kisses on her cheek as they viewed the art. Her legs were long, toned, smooth and oiled, walking inside of black four inch stilettos.

"Thank you baby." Essence replied, while wrapping her arms around him, and planting a soft kiss on his cheek. They were standing in front of a painting of a night view of Chicago's city skyline. The water in Lake Michigan was still and there was a white yacht, with yellow lights in the windows, that gave the water no choice but to repel the light. "You're welcome sweetheart. I love you." he said, hugging her again. "I love you too Isaiah."

The competition was about to begin and the host, Zoe Brice could be seen picking up a microphone to welcome the guest.

"Good afternoon everyone! My name is Zoe Brice, and I am the owner of The Painting Palace and your host! I hope our competitors are ready to showcase their art and I hope you all enjoy what they've worked so very hard to create."

Zoe was a short, petite caramel skinned woman with a taper fade haircut that had a lining better than most men. She wore canary yellow wide-legged dress pants, with a white, front button, sleeveless, slim fitting, down collared shirt. Her shoes were all white six inch ankle strapped, open toed heels, exposing her white polished pedicured toes.

"At this moment, I am going to ask all of our competitors to remove the cloth that is concealing your painting."

As all of the teen competitors began removing their cloth from their canvas, the guests were clapping and cheering them on. There had to be at least 200 people present. Noa saw her family front and center to view her piece. "One by one, each competitor will state their name, their age, grade, and the name of their piece. Then, they will explain the inspiration behind their artwork in a few short sentences. Once all of the competitors present, each guest will have the opportunity to observe each painting and cast a vote for a winner on their phone by going to the gallery's website, and clicking on art competition 2024, and choosing an artist. First up, we have Mr. Quincy Reynolds."

"Hi everyone, my name is Quincy. I'm a sophomore and I'm fifteen years old." He had a painting of a boulder, sitting in a large puddle, in the middle of a sandy beach, on a hot summer day. Surrounding the boulder were beach goers who played volleyball, built sandcastles, ate homemade sandwiches from their coolers, and lounged around on lawn chairs or blankets, tanning. It was an oil painting, and he explained that he's always felt like the oddball in his friend groups, and the kid who was always perceived as different from the rest. He believed that a boulder sitting in still water in the middle of sand on the beach represented his theory about himself. He said, "I've always remained still and composed any time someone's perception of me threatened my self-esteem and confidence. The rock represents me, the oddball, and the water it sits in represents my calm temperament. The beach goers depict everyone else who continues to move forward with life with or without me around. Therefore, I remain still and confident in my differences, never allowing anyone to deter me from my true self, based on their own perceptions. I call this piece, *Be Still.*"

After Quincy was a senior girl, Monica, who had a watercolor painting of uneven patterns of warm reds and cold blues, some orange, and a hint of yellow. In the center of the patterns was a little girl and her teddy bear, sitting Indian style, her head down, chin pressed into her chest. She was embracing her bear tightly. Her two pigtails were stiff and had a tiny white bow at the end of each braid. Monica informed the audience that she was diagnosed with autism spectrum disorder, and oftentimes she feels misunderstood just like the uneven patterns in her painting. "No matter how beautiful the colors are, it's still imperfect. The little girl sits there, waiting to be accepted by society, and not shunned for her disability. I call this piece, *Composed Chaos.*

Next, it was Noa's turn. She was nervous because some of the competitors who presented before her were exceptional. She was impressed and nonetheless inspired by their work. She studied her audience before she spoke. There was a delicacy to her elegance that emanated from her confidence. For some inexplicable reason, even unbeknownst to Noa, she realized and understood exactly who she was at that very moment. She stood on the left side of her painting, took a deep breath, and began.

"Good afternoon everyone. My name is Noa Jackson. I'm sixteen and a junior at Southside High. The name of my piece is called *He said He Wouldn't Hurt Me.* I chose this title because the woman in my photo represents all the women who have been hurt by someone, especially the man she loved. Her eyes tell stories of women's pain, and her long, flowing hair, houses the burden of having to remain elegant, poised, and respectable, even when all she wants to do is break down. Her lips are slightly open because sometimes, we as women want to tell someone about the pain we're enduring, only we have realized, the people we want to tell, are the same ones we can't trust. She's attempting to wipe away a tear, because women have always had to remain strong, no matter the depth of their afflictions, discomforts, and suffering. My dad left home when I was eleven years old, and my sister Harper was nine. He was the first man to hurt me, at one point in a way I thought was beyond forgiving. I heard my mother's cries late at night, and the times she'd be sick, vomiting bile in the bathroom because she couldn't eat for days, or sleep for weeks. Through it all, my mother remained graceful and strong, despite her pain. I admire her for that. This painting is a delineation of every woman who has been hurt by a man who told her he never would, and still had to carry herself with decency, decorum, and respectability. He said he'd never hurt me, but he did anyway. Thank you."

The audience roared with applause, whistling, cheering, and congratulating Noa. Essence and Harper wiped tears from their eyes, and embraced Noa together. "I'm so proud of you Noa. You are so beautiful and talented, and I'm just so grateful to be your mom." She held onto Noa for some time, seemingly mentally reverting back to memories of Noa being born and running around as a toddler. She remembered Noa's first steps, and the first time she called Essence ma-ma. She recalled Noa's first painting that she displayed on the freezer in the kitchen and how excited Noa was to see it every day. Her unwavering support for Noa was apparent. "Great job." Essence whispered again, as Noa returned to her canvas.

After the last competitor presented, Zoe approached the microphone. "Alright everyone! Let's give our artists another round of applause. Those were amazing pieces right?!" The audience cheered in agreement. "Right now, is the time where everyone can take a few moments and observe the artists' pieces before casting their vote. In thirty minutes, I will announce the winner of the art competition.

"Those paintings don't stand a chance against yours Noa." Harper said. "I have to agree, that was pretty deep." Emmett added.

"Thank you. I was so nervous up there. But I'm proud of myself."

"You should be. Picasso who?!" Essence smiled.

The votes were in, and each artist stood next to their painting. "I have the final votes.. Before I announce the winner, I want you all to know that your work is remarkable, and you all have bright futures ahead of you." There was a big projection screen beginning to roll down on the wall behind the artists. "On this screen, the name of the winner will be displayed, along with their art. I also forgot to mention that whoever wins, I will personally purchase and hang their canvas in my gallery."

The audience grew silent as the contestants viewed the blank screen behind them. Noa's palms began to sweat, and she swallowed the lump of nervousness in her throat that almost made her choke.

"And the winner is..." The screen lit up behind the artists. It unveiled *Noa Hope Jackson: He Said He'd Never Hurt Me.*

"Oh my God! I won! Ma look I won! I really won!" she screamed. Noa burst into tears and fell to her knees. Essence and Isaiah ran over to her, helping her to her feet and consoled her. She hugged Essence tightly, and then Isaiah. "Thank you for coming today Isaiah. It means a lot." she said, wiping away tears. "No problem Noa. Thank you for inviting us."

Zoe Brice approached Noa with a check for five thousand dollars, a ten thousand dollar scholarship to the art school of her choice, and a folder with paperwork for an all-inclusive seven day, six night vacation to Disney World. She also handed her another check for three thousand dollars for the purchase of her artwork.

"Oh my God! Thank you so much! I can't believe it! Thank you!" she cried.

Essence watched as other guests congratulated Noa, patting her on the back, and giving her hugs. She smiled, knowing Noa would be just fine moving forward.

Chapter 17

School had finally let out for the summer and Noa and Harper couldn't wait to go to Disney World. Essence planned for them to go the week after school was over. Isaiah decided to purchase tickets for he and Emmett, since Essence extended an invite. "Will you be able to take off work for a whole week? Essence asked concerned. "I'll be fine sweetheart. Don't worry about me. We'd love to go with you all."

The Saturday before they left for Disney World, Isaiah offered to take Essence and the girls to dinner. Underneath a clear and starry sky, the night was pleasant and warm with a refreshing breeze that swept through soothingly and peacefully. Before they went to dinner, he said he needed to make a stop first. "It's something I want to show you Essence." She was puzzled. She looked in the backseat at Noa and Harper, who both shrugged their shoulders with confused faces. He drove to the old furniture store that now had a huge sign on the top of the building that read: *Isaiah's Impact.* The signage was decorated in powder blue letters, with a black outline. The building was repainted into a tan color with off white frosted glass double doors.

"You bought the building?! I thought you were just working for someone to install the electrical wiring." Essence remarked astonishingly.

"I did and I was. I work for myself, Essence. I own the company I work for. I started *Lights the Bright Way Electrical Company* after my divorce. It's been thriving since." he replied. "I've been working on the electrical work for this building, because it was something I purchased, and I wanted to be a part of remodeling it."

"That's incredible Isaiah! I'm so happy for you!" She glared at the sign again. There were little white lights on both sides of the building that lit the sidewalk daily once the sun retreated, and the moon surfaced.

"Thank you sweetheart. But it's still something else I want you to see. Come on."

They all got out of the car and Essence noticed Noa and Harper giggling amongst each other. They whispered to each other things Essence couldn't really make out and kept giggling.

"Girls, what's going on?"

"We really don't know ma." Noa laughed. They followed Isaiah into the building. When he turned on the lights, Essence gasped. Past the secretary's desk, into an open space were green, blue, yellow, and red circular tables with four chairs sitting around each of them. There were multicolored cups of pencils and pens on each table and composition books. The floors were mostly hardwood, with individual beige carpeting throughout. There were lounging chairs and bean bag chairs in the corners, ten brand new computers stationed against the wall, and a bookcase filled with classic literature, children's books, urban novels, and more. Right above the bookcase was a sign that read: *The Essence of Writing*.

"Is this for me?!" Essence shrieked.

Isaiah moved closer to her, placing a hand on each one of her cheeks. He kissed her forehead and said, "The first day we met, you told me you wanted to open up an after school program for aspiring writers. I knew I had just purchased this building a few months prior and thought it would be the perfect place for something like that."

"You thought enough of me in that way after meeting me once?"

"It was something about the sincerity in your voice when you said it. I knew you meant it. It wasn't until I really got to know you that I decided I wanted to turn it into a place for your program."

Essence began to weep. She glared at Noa and Harper who were smiling from ear to ear. "You all knew about this?" she asked. "He made us promise not to tell you ma." Harper laughed. Essence kneeled down and hugged Noa and Essence, sobbing into their arms. They hugged her back firmly. "Ma, look. Turn around." Noa whispered.

Essence returned to her feet and turned around to see Isaiah down on one knee. "Oh my God Isaiah! Oh my God! Oh my God! Is this for real?! Are you for real?!" she shouted in excitement.

"Essence, I love you so much. I love your daughters, and I want to be a sense of unfaltering peace in your life that heats your heart and calms the storms in your life. I want to bring smiles upon your face daily, and comfort you with ease on your hardest days. I think about you when I wake up in the morning, and I'm at peace knowing you are alright in my arms. I want to protect you from anything that emerges meant to stifle you and bring you pain. You are the epitome of grace, beauty and sophistication and I want you next to me as I continue walking through this life. Essence, my love for you transcends beyond the boundaries of dialect and cliche phrases about love, embodying an affection for you so intense and profound, that no words, no matter how beautifully placed together could ever fully convey. Essence Olivia Jackson, will you marry me?"

She was frozen, and her heart raced with happiness a million miles a second. Her hands covered her mouth, and her stomach felt those same butterflies they felt when Isaiah turned around at the bar that first night. The overwhelming feeling of shock, disbelief, and then pure bliss.

"Yes! Yes! I'll marry you!" she screamed as he placed the ring on her finger. She pulled him to his feet, and they exchanged the most passionate kiss that brought tears to Noa and Harper's eyes. Seeing their mom getting proposed to made them happy and excited for her.

"Did you all know he was going to propose?!" Essence asked excitedly.

"Yea. He talked to us about it weeks ago." Noa answered. "He made us promise not to tell you."

"Oh, Isaiah. Thank you so much for the after school program and everything that you have done for me. I love you so much!"

"I love you too, sweetheart."

When they all returned from Disney World, Essence went to visit Dr. Reed.

"How are you Essence?"

She raised her left hand showing the diamond ring Isaiah planted on her finger.

"Oh my God he proposed?!"

"He sure did, right before we went to Disney World."

"I am so happy for you Essence. That is beautiful."

"That's not all. He's the one that bought the old furniture building. He called it *Isaiah's Impact* and designed an entire after school program for aspiring writers for me."

"He did?!" Dr. Reed shouted.

"He sure did. He called the program, *The Essence of Writing.*"

"Wow, he really loves you! I love this for you Essence. How is everything else?"

"Everything is good. For the first time in my life, I feel like I can finally breathe. I'm not so overwhelmed, and I'm putting my mental health first now. I haven't spoken to my mother since the conversation and the letter I sent her. I'm ok with it though. I know that I love her, and I know that she's human, as am I. However, I've learned that in order to receive the love I believe I deserve, I must first give it to myself. Waiting on someone to love me correctly is such an unhealthy way of thinking, that it began to dismantle my emotional stability. My mother may not have protected me during one of the darkest times in my life and showed me the care and affection that I yearned for from her, however, I appreciate her for raising me and instilling in me the fortitude to continue thriving despite any hindrance or obstacle. I'm on a healing journey that will take time, patience, and understanding, and that is what I'm giving myself. Motherhood is hard. Experiencing it with my own children is a task in itself. However, I relish in it, knowing that the times where I may fall short, or my kids, I remain objective to their wants, needs, and desires, without making it about me. I listen to them. I give them grace and ingrain the idea of maintaining respect and love for each other, and protecting one another, never allowing anyone to come between them. I'm learning daily Dr. Reed. I'm growing, and I'm healing. Trauma, whether it's mental, emotional, or sexual, traveled through generation after generation in my family, and I chose to break the cycle of toxicity, secrets, jealousy, harshness, and neglectful behavior."

"Wow Essence. I'm very proud of you. I love this journey you're venturing off into."

"Thank you Dr. Reed."

Essence left her therapy session smiling and free. She drove past *Isaiah's Impact* on her way home and her eyes beamed while she grinned from ear to ear. She knew deep down in her heart that from that day forward, life for her, Noa and Harper was going to be better than it ever was before.

Made in the USA
Monee, IL
26 May 2025

18144891R00100